DOROTHY ED

(1903 – 1934) was born at Ogmore Vale, Glamorgan in Wales, the daughter of a poor schoolmaster who claimed to be a descendant of Nell Gwyn. A pioneering socialist and friend of Keir Hardie, he brought up Dorothy as a strict vegetarian, and she became a lifelong member of the Independent Labour Party. At the age of nine, dressed entirely in red, she welcomed Keir Hardie on to the platform of a meeting during the Welsh miners' strike at Tonypandy in 1912. Dorothy Edwards was also an ardent Welsh Nationalist, although she could not speak Welsh.

Dorothy was educated at the boys' school where her father taught, and then at University College, Cardiff where she took a degree in Greek and philosophy. She read French, Italian, German and Norwegian literature, and in particular the Russians. An accomplished singer, her passion for music took her to Vienna for six months where she lived with a socialist bookseller and his wife, teaching them English in return for her board and lodging. She also lived in Florence for nine months, travelling extensively in Italy. Following her father's death, she and her mother, a Christian Scientist, moved to the village of Rhiwbina on the outskirts of Cardiff. Dorothy was determined not to become a teacher, so the household depended largely on her mother's small salary as a teacher, and later her pension.

The first story Dorothy Edwards ever tried to publish was included in Edward O'Brien's *Best Short Stories*. Her stories were published in British and American magazines, and collected into one volume, *Rhapsody*, in 1927. Its admirers included Arnold Bennett and Gerald Gould, who spoke of her as a writer of genius. Raymond Mortimer suggested to David Garnett that he read *Rhapsody* and Garnett later wrote in his auto-biography, 'Raymond was right. The stories were peculiarly to my taste and, what is more, revealed an entirely original talent. I was greatly excited and wrote to the authoress.' They met in 1929, a year after the publication of her novel, *Winter Sonata*, which Gerald Brenan acclaimed for its 'special flavour that is unlike anything else'.

She became friends with David and Ray Garnett, living with them, in 1933, in their Endsleigh Street house in London. The Garnetts took her to stay with Lytton Strachey at Hamspray, and introduced her to Virginia Woolf, Duncan Grant, Vanessa Bell, Theodore Powys, Carrington, Clive Bell and Roger Fry. But Dorothy found she could not write any better in London than in Wales, and returned to her mother's home. On the morning of 6th January 1934 she burnt her letters and papers; that afternoon she threw herself under a train. A note was found in her pocket which is thought to have read 'I have received kindnesses from many people, but I have not really loved any human being.'

RHAPSODY

DOROTHY EDWARDS

WITH A NEW INTRODUCTION BY
ELAINE MORGAN

PENGUIN BOOKS – VIRAGO PRESS

PENGUIN BOOKS
Viking Penguin Inc., 40 West 23rd Street,
New York, New York 10010, U.S.A.
Penguin Books Ltd, Harmondsworth,
Middlesex, England
Penguin Books Australia Ltd, Ringwood,
Victoria, Australia
Penguin Books Canada Limited, 2801 John Street,
Markham, Ontario, Canada L3R 1B4
Penguin Books (N.Z.) Ltd, 182–190 Wairau Road,
Auckland 10, New Zealand

First published in Great Britain by Wishart & Co. 1927
First published in the United States of America by
Alfred A. Knopf, Inc., 1928
This edition first published in Great Britain by
Virago Press Limited 1986
Published in Penguin Books 1986

Printed in Great Britain
by Anchor Brendon Ltd, Tiptree, Essex

To

MR. FRED. STIBBS

NOTE

SOME of these stories were first published in *The Calendar*, and " A Country House " was included in *The Best Short Stories* of 1926.

CONTENTS

INTRODUCTION

DOROTHY EDWARDS was born in 1903, the loved and only child of an idealistic Welshman who claimed to be descended not from Charles II—he was too egalitarian to boast of that—but from Nell Gwyn. A pioneering Shavian, socialist and vegetarian, he had glimpsed the imminent dawn of a new and better age when all men—and women, too—would live together in peace and comradeship; and Dorothy's early upbringing was apparently designed to fit her for life in that brave new world. For her first eleven years he allowed her, according to some accounts, to "run wild" among the gangs of village lads from the boys' school in which he was Headmaster, and in which Dorothy herself was educated. (According to her own account she became the leader of one such gang.)

He passed on to her his passionate love of books and his vision of the coming Revolution. She often recalled being dressed in scarlet at the age of nine to welcome Keir Hardie onto the platform during the Tonypandy miners' strike; others remember her as a schoolgirl at left-wing rallies in Cardiff, thrillingly declaiming poems from William Morris.

Her first taste of a more conventional edu-

cation was at Howell's School, Cardiff. She
found it hard to bend her neck to the pedagogic
yoke, but that was more of a headache to her
teachers than to herself, and as a twelve-year-
old tomboy she was something of a heroine to
her peers. They were halcyon days which in
later life she would describe with a passionate
nostalgia which puzzled and sometimes bored
her listeners. Perhaps it was the last time she
was really happy. For, unfortunately, Mr
Edwards had miscalculated, and the coming
utopia was unaccountably delayed. After his
death his darling daughter was left to adjust to a
world in which class distinctions and sexual
divisions were as rigid as ever; and in ado-
lescence it is rather late to begin to learn to be a
woman as womanhood was then understood.
Dorothy never completely internalised the
"feminine" role. Whenever she writes a story in
the first person it is a man who is the narrator.
She once wrote: "Women like sybils, with
strength like iron, do not exist any more. Goddesses are now wisps of things."

She herself was not a wisp of a thing. She
was, according to her friends, a pretty girl who
grew into a lovely woman. "Her lips were often
parted owing to her projecting teeth (they were
beautiful teeth)—the general effect being most
attractive." Ardent, eager, vivacious, clear-

skinned, a fresh complexion, bright eyes and luxuriant hair—all observers are agreed on these details. But her figure is variously described by her friends in Wales as "well built" or "well proportioned"; a colder English eye, comparing her to the willowy ladies of Bloomsbury, was reminded of a "healthy young Jersey heifer".

There were many young men who paid court to her, and there were several men whose qualities of mind or character she passionately admired; but the only engagement—to a College lecturer—was quickly broken. The admired ones were all safely married, or father-figures, or half a world away, or otherwise unobtainable. Dorothy had not been reared to dwindle into a wife.

In the class hierarchy, as in the sexual one, she found herself curiously adrift. Her heart was romantically committed to the workers, but once her father's aegis was removed she found it difficult to relate to them. In Wales the socialist powerhouse was up in the Valleys, spearheaded by the miners' unions, where parlour-pink females with educated "English" voices like Dorothy's carried no weight. Moreover, her widowed mother had moved from Ogmore to a respectable Cardiff suburb, and Dorothy's only practical way of helping the miners was by trekking over the Caerphilly

mountain to Senghenydd and seeking out the
most needy cases to distribute medical supplies
and secondhand clothing. She tried hard, but
felt acutely miscast in this charitable rôle.

Her grasp of dialectics was never more than
tenuous. She once joined Harold Watkins's
evening classes on the Gold Standard because
"gold is such a brilliant, beautiful colour", and
one suspects she valued politics partly for its
ability to stoke up the temperature of general conversation. She was never very good at small talk.

At University College, Cardiff, she seems to
have been both popular and hard working. She
contributed flippant, self-derisive little essays
to the College magazine. Literature she read for
pleasure—not only the English novelists but
also French, Italian, German, Norwegian and
especially the Russian ones. She took her degree
in Greek and Philosophy.

After that she lost her way. It was a truth
universally acknowledged that a young woman
of above average brains and only average looks,
living in Cardiff with a widowed mother, was
designed by Providence to become a teacher.
Her mother and all her friends pleaded with
her to bow to this destiny. Even after her
untimely death they mourned: If only she had
become a teacher, she might have been with us
today. It may well have been true.

But Dorothy was her father's daughter, raised in the faith that something high and gallant lay ahead for those who had the courage to grasp it. Like any E.M. Forster heroine, she quitted the damp, Bible-black climate of Glamorgan and headed for the warm South. She was given six months' hospitality by the family of a Viennese socialist bookseller in return for teaching them English; by some other unrecorded ploy she contrived nine months in Florence, soaking up beauty and learning about life and art. Then she came home to live in Rhiwbina on her mother's pittance of a pension and her own earnings as a freelance writer. Those earnings were very meagre. She was philosophical about this, freely accepting that publishers were not in the game for their health; but she for her part was not in it primarily for the money. She persisted in doing her own thing, regardless of the state of the market.

"An author Dorothy wants to be, you know," Mrs Edwards rather helplessly informed her friends. The pair of them settled for a life on the edge of poverty while this ideal was being pursued, and the mother was consoled by being accompanied twice a week to the cinema, where she revelled in escapist romance while her daughter earnestly analysed "the scenarios" and dreamed of one day scripting a film that would go down in history.

The stories she was actually writing were curiously gentle and low-keyed. By this time, inspired by Saunders Lewis whom she knew personally and revered as a very great man, she was calling herself a (non-Welsh-speaking) Welsh Nationalist, as well as a socialist. Devotion to these two brave causes filled her conversation with fire and passion, but none of that was reflected in her fiction. Some people found her stories miniscule and precious. One disappointed local reviewer complained that the writing "lacks spontaneity. We wonder if the author has ever screamed."

He was wrong on that score, but the mistake was understandable. The likelihood is that her own emotional experiences at that time were far too raw and unassimilated to be allowed to surface. Perhaps she feared that if she allowed herself to scream, the scream would have been too loud for dignity or comfort.

The year 1927 was a good one for her. She was twenty-four, and a collection of her short stories from English and American magazines published in that year was a *succès d'estime* in both countries. Gerald Gould in the *Observer* hailed her as a genius; she was acclaimed as one of the three great writers of the year. Dorothy began to blossom and to let her hair down— quite literally: she unpinned the modest bun of hair at her nape and walked around Rhiwbina with blonde tresses flowing down to her waist, an unheard-of fashion in those days. She enjoyed her local celebrity; on return visits to the University, wearing a dashing cloak and gesturing with a long ivory cigarette holder, she would be immediately surrounded by admiring students.

Above all, the London literati had now become aware of her existence, and after the publication of her second book in 1928 she began to meet them. She was invited to meet David and Ray Garnett, and later to stay with them and accompany them when they went on holiday. Ray Garnett got on very well with Dorothy. David, although saying "she was one of the very few young women for whom I felt absolutely no sexual attraction at all", admired her literary talents, and possibly her ardent appreciation of his own. "Sometime around 1930," he wrote, "I asked her in a letter if she was willing to adopt me as her brother, and allow me to adopt her as a sister . . . Ray thought I was being silly, and no doubt she was right."

But the compact was made, and the intermittent visits continued. It was gratifying to the Garnetts to be able to introduce the "Welsh Cinderella" to the kind of luxuries she had never been accustomed to: a glass of wine, a ride in a private car, a seat in the stalls of the theatre, an introduction to such literary lions as Lytton Strachey, Duncan Grant, Vanessa Bell, Theodore Powys . . . A few years later, when Dorothy was anxious to escape from her mother's increasingly querulous company and the Garnett's young son William was being troubled by night fears, they installed her in their attic as a combination of literary protegée and resident baby sitter.

Something went badly wrong. Dorothy, misled by the talk of sisterhood, had always failed to appreciate all the nuances of her Cinderella status. She tended to behave as if the world of letters was a genuine republic—as if here at least the age of equality had already arrived. She was presuming a little too much. After being introduced to Virginia Woolf, "who", writes Garnett, "seemed vague but full of friendly astonishment," Dorothy was felt to have been insufficiently impressed and to have talked too freely about herself—a grave solecism. When a young airman came to lunch and held forth about the ancient Greeks, Dorothy "interrupted him without ceremony". (After all, she had graduated in Greek and must have imagined her views had some validity.) "She was a bit vexed when we told her he was Colonel Lawrence of Arabia and we, on our part, were considerably surprised that she needed to be told."

Young William continued to adore her, but David Garnett began to find the proximity of his adopted sister increasingly intolerable. He became less admiring of her "ardent and passionate directness, her fresh and individual mind" and more irritated by "her clumsy homemade dresses and her lack of any form of corset". Dorothy shrivelled in the draught of his repugnance, and unhappiness made her neurotic. Her hair was now screwed up more uncompromisingly than ever in its schoolmarm bun; the typewriter in her attic tapped more sporadically, and finally came to a halt.

Dorothy Parker spent a lifetime flirting with the thought of suicide and declaring that she knew when she was going to die. Dorothy Edwards only said it once. She went home to Wales, left a note in the pocket of her mackintosh, and threw herself under a train. She was thirty-one, and the Revolution still had not arrived. It was nobody's fault.

In the stories in this collection Dorothy ignored the cardinal rule commended to all beginners: "Write about what you know best." None of these characters ever lived in a Cardiff suburb or worried about money or made their own clothes; none allowed pugnacious intellectual concepts about socialism or nationalism to quicken their pulses; some of them suffered, but never to the torture point of seeking their own quietus on a railway line.

She wrote instead about a leisurely world of country houses and unearned incomes and tea parties, as English as Cranford or Howard's End. It was not the real England; indeed, it was not quite the real world. It was a landscape created out of her own mind.

The style, too, was a conscious artefact, quite different from the fluent elliptic English she used in her letters. It is an extremely plain and simple language, though it is often used to say very subtle things. Sometimes it is fleetingly reminiscent of another writer. The echo is an elusive one, and when it is tracked down is rather embarrassing. But the truth must be faced: now and again in the early tales (as in the title story where the excitable Mr Everett urges a chance-met stranger to "come and stay with us for a few days"), we are not a million miles from Mr Salteena and *The Young Visiters*. And in some respects Dorothy's world continued to be described with an eye as innocent as young Daisy Ashford's.

The child Daisy could well have written, for example, the description of Mr Wendover carrying three brown eggs as a gift for his hostess "very carefully, two in one hand and one in the other. People who passed him, especially people in charabancs, laughed at him, though there was really nothing to laugh about." And she might easily have pondered, concerning another character who always wore a hat too small for him "as though he never looked in a mirror with his hat on—and yet surely he did when he bought it".

When she wrote those paragraphs Dorothy Edwards had not yet got it right. She seems to have been consciously trying to pare away the cultural accretions of the disillusioned years and to see the world again in the clear light that had shone on it when she was twelve, or thereabouts. Some people found the effect odd and *faux naïf*, and in the beginning sometimes it was. But quite soon she learned to eradicate that element without losing the freshness and directness she was aiming at, and by the end of this collection she had discovered her own voice and her own perspective.

Music features strongly in most of her stories. Dorothy Edwards had been given singing lessons by a first-class professional tutor. Music, like teaching, was frequently recommended to her as a more practical way of earning a living than writing her off-beat stories. She uses music, and people's response to it, as a touchstone of their characters.

Frederick, in *The Conquered*, is half enthralled by the glamorous Gwyneth, but later, from the way she sings a Welsh folk song and even more from the way she refuses to sing a Polish one, he deduces that she belongs on the other side of the invisible watershed dividing the human race into winners and losers. She cannot do justice to the lament of the subjugated Poles because "she would have been on the side of the conquerors . . . When I looked at Gwyneth again, it seemed to me that some of her beauty had gone."

Throughout this collection it is the women who have their feet firmly on the ground; the men tend to be more romantic and less sure of themselves, observing the females with anxious attention like men in a Thurber cartoon, wondering what they are up to. This relationship is exploited to comic effect in the story called *Summer-Time*. Mr Joseph Laurel, on a visit to a country house, becomes deeply interested in a red-haired schoolgirl more than twenty years his junior. He is totally mystified by the little smiles of malice and veiled amusement cast at him by his old friend Beatrice. When the girl walks away with her boy friend and Mr Laurel's youth vanishes with them, he is suddenly struck by the appalled realisation of why Beatrice had been amused, and why there had been malice in it, and why when he played tennis with her "balls seemed to be hurled at him from every direction, and every one of them seemed to be expressing contempt".

The stories seldom have so predictable an outcome. Even a single sentence is liable to change direction in the middle and not end up where it seemed to be heading for. "She was certainly rather pretty . . . When she spoke or looked up at anyone there was something naïve and childlike about her which Ferris entirely failed to find beautiful or even interesting." Mr Ferris is not one of the tentative male types. When Elizabeth asks him for the loan of a book, he pompously reflects that "most women only talk about reading, and that is merely the preliminary to talking about love". So we know he is an ass, and wait for him to get his come-uppance, as Jane Austen's Mr Collins did at the hands of another Elizabeth. But life is not that simple, and even pompous asses are sometimes right, and all she wanted was to corner him in a tower and press herself against him and be kissed.

Some of the best portraits are of outsiders— predictably, for Dorothy was an outsider all her life. Sometimes they are lonely men who hover for a while on the periphery of an unhappy marriage until the husband grows uneasy and finds some wordless way of pulling up the drawbridge; in one case he even underlines his territorial claims by hoisting a flag. Once it is a husband who is tempted and his wife who sees the danger signals, but again the ranks are closed, and the stranger is excluded. If the writer identified herself with these solitary figures it is possibly significant that none of them genuinely had the will to win, only to warm themselves for a while at someone else's hearth.

She was constructing a world as individual, as internally consistent, as L.S. Lowry's landscapes or the novels of Henry James or Ivy Compton Burnett. The trouble is that these concepts take time to mature, and even more time to impose themselves upon the public consciousness. If any of those artists had lived for only thirty-one years the chances are that their names would have sunk, as hers has done, into almost total oblivion.

Elaine Morgan,
Glamorgan, 1986

RHAPSODY

Last summer, on the very first day I returned from Egypt for my summer vacation, I made a new and interesting acquaintance. I reached London at about three o'clock, and had to wait about until a six-o'clock appointment with my firm, and because I was too tired to do anything else in the meantime, and feeling also a little depressed and lonely, I turned into a café and sat there drinking tea and reading a magazine. At about four a man walked in and sat at the table in front of mine. He was short and thin, with very straight fair hair and pale blue eyes, and he was perhaps about forty years of age, though he looked very young. His face wore a curious expression, as if he were listening all the time to something intensely illuminating but scarcely audible, or as if he were experiencing some almost intolerably sweet emotion, and he seemed to be imploring you "Please don't interrupt me for a moment; it will soon be over."

I noticed him particularly as he ordered tea and poured it out for himself, and I remember thinking what a neat and well-ordered personality he must be.

Then I went back to my magazine, and, when next I looked up, he was standing at my side,

I

trying to attract my attention by saying in a very polite voice, "Pardon me, could you tell me what time it is?"

The fact of his not knowing the time was so much out of harmony with the conception I had formed of his "well-ordered personality," and I was so muddle-headed after my rather sensational magazine story, that I did a very rude thing. I said, "But haven't you a watch?"

He put two fingers into his watch-pocket and said, "No. I lent it to my little boy this morning. It has been a great inconvenience all day."

"It is a quarter to five," I said hurriedly; and then, to make up for my rudeness, I offered him a cigarette, and asked him if he would not sit down at my table. He accepted my invitation very politely, and sat down.

"It is most unpleasant being without a watch," he said seriously. "I am so anxious not to miss my train, which goes at 5.40, because my wife is an invalid. There was no means of ascertaining the time at the concert this afternoon, and I regret to say that I came out of it earlier than necessary, because I thought it was later than it actually was. That is why I have some time to spend here."

"Yes. That is awfully annoying," I said.

"However," and his expression of intolerable bliss returned, "I heard a great deal."

"You are fond of music?" I remarked.

"Yes," he answered. "I never have the opportunity to hear very much now. It is impossible for me to come to town in the evening, because I cannot get home the same night. I can never go to the opera, for instance, though I am very fond of Mozart. My wife is an invalid, so that I do not like to leave her for very long. She used to play, but our tastes were dissimilar in many ways, and now she cannot play at all."

"And do you not play?" I asked.

"Alas, no!" he answered. "I can finger out the notes in a very clumsy way, but though that gives me pleasure, I am sure it causes great anguish to everyone anywhere near, and it annoys my wife terribly, because her technique was always excellent. I can see you are sympathising with me," he added almost gaily. "I suppose you can play beautifully. Is that so?"

I laughed too. "No," I said. "I am very fond of music, though. I quite understand how you must miss it."

He was delighted. He began to hum the little Minueto from *Don Giovanni* ecstatically in a whisper. Suddenly he said, "But, though you do not play, you will go to hear everything this season while I shall hear nothing."

I was so anxious to take away some of his envy that I answered sorrowfully, "Yes, but

3

even if it were possible to go to concerts every day, it is very dull wandering about by oneself in between for a whole three months."

He was all compassion. "You have no friends here? Perhaps you do not live in London?"

It seemed a pity to talk about me, but I had made it inevitable.

"I have a job in Egypt—Alexandria," I said. "I am home for three months, and there is nothing particularly to do now except go to theatres. I do not know what I shall do in August."

"It is a pity you do not play," he said, appearing not to have listened to what I said. "You will be sorry some day. When I was a boy I had a sister who played everything for me, and then my wife was a beautiful pianist, so I never practised myself. Now, of course, I can't begin playing scales with an invalid in the house. Perhaps you sing, though?" he added suspiciously.

I blushed a little. "I used to have a bit of a voice," I admitted.

He drummed on the table with his little finger. Then suddenly he stopped, and a most cunning expression pirouetted across his face. He looked up and said casually, "Perhaps, if you are indeed without engagements, you would care to

4

spend a few days with me. We are going away
in a fortnight's time, so that it would have to be
before then." And a little less casually he added:
"Do you think you could possibly sing un-
accompanied?" and really there was a most
pathetically imploring expression in his eyes.

So I said yes at once, and promised to stay
with him the very next week. Then I had to
remind him of the time, and, flinging his card
down on the table, he scurried away, waving his
new grey gloves in an ecstatic farewell. And I
was left, somewhat to my own astonishment, with
an engagement on my hands. However, I continued in that mood of loneliness when one is
quite ready to take a passionate interest in the
affairs of any stranger, so the next week I went
down to see him. He lived in the country, some
way out of London. He seemed altogether delighted to see me, and even more delighted to
see some music under my arm. With great
restraint he did not mention the music, only he
put it reverently on the hall-table. Then we
went in to tea. His wife was rather disappoint-
ing. She lay on a sofa presiding over the tea-
table, though Everett himself actually poured
out the tea. She was a dark, thick-set woman,
with large, heavy white hands. Her face bore
the marks of much physical suffering, so that
she looked older than her husband, though

suppose she was about the same age, and she wore an expression which was neither complaint nor resignation, but something quite different from either. I liked her at once, though of course she did not strike my imagination as her husband did.

"George said you were finding England lonely," she said.

I smiled, thinking that I had been represented to her simply as an object of compassion.

"Oh, not very seriously," I said. "Only I had been looking forward to getting here, and forgot that there would be no one to meet me. Your husband found me in the middle of that mood. Now I am quite reconciled to being at the centre of the earth instead of at its outskirts."

"Yes," she said slowly. "I never go to town now."

Everett said excitably, "Please have a cress sandwich. I grow them myself in boxes on the window-ledge."

It was exceedingly pleasant to be welcomed with such enthusiasm, even though I knew the cunning that lay beneath it. Mrs Everett seemed glad to see me too. I suppose she saw few people, as they lived in the country. I found them both very interesting. It was curious how, whenever Everett mentioned music, he looked at her a little apprehensively, and she almost imperceptibly frowned. I wonder if she had awakened one day to find that he had married her because she was a beautiful pianist, and perhaps she took a dislike to music from that day?

During tea their little son came into the room. He was a nice little chap, with dark eyes like his mother's. He shook hands with me shyly and said to Everett:

"Please, father, will you lend me your watch again to-morrow?"

"Oh yes, Vincent, certainly," said his father, with great attentiveness.

"Why do you want it?" asked his mother heavily.

"Well, the truf is," said he, "I showed it to Dick last week, and he told another little boy that I had one, so I had better show it to the other little boy to-morrow."

"All right," said his mother; "go and play now."

"You won't forget, father?" said Vincent.

"No," said Everett. "I cannot give it to you now, because I am going to take Mr Elliott for a walk, and we will not know when it is time for dinner, but you shall have it immediately afterwards."

"I have a watch, you know," I said.

7

"Oh, then in that case Vincent can have it now." And he took out of his pocket a very magnificent gold watch and gave it to the boy. Vincent put it carefully into his trousers-pocket and then went out.

"Nice little chap," I said.

"Yes," said his mother. "He is going away to school in September. When you take Mr Elliott out, George, go along to the woods; he will like that best."

"Yes," said Everett. "I hope you are not feeling tired now. Is there anything I can do for you?"

"No, thank you," she said, without looking up.

Everett led me outside, and we began to walk along a road shaded by trees. He had the air of one about to impart a desperate secret.

"I have been so anxious to tell you," he said. "I have evolved a scheme. Next week we are going to Scotland for a holiday."

"But can Mrs Everett travel so far?" I asked in surprise.

"Oh yes," he said quickly. "She likes it there very much. We will go all the way by car. It is expensive, but of course it will be better for her than going by train. We stay at a place called Glen Elan, and the man who lives in the cottage we stay at plays the violin—not very

8

well, you know, but he has a quite natural talent for it."

"Oh, I see."

"The piano there is an old one, but I have already written to get it tuned before we arrive. But this is the scheme that I have on foot. Vincent is going to school in September. Now, do you not think he should have a governess during these two months? I don't want him to be behind the other boys in his studies."

"I think it would perhaps be a good thing," I said cautiously.

He beamed at me. "And she would keep him from worrying his mother, and give the maid the opportunity to devote all her time to her."

"Yes."

"Well, do you know what I have done?" he said, and his wisp of a voice rose to a crescendo of excitement. "I put a carefully worded advertisement in the paper. I asked for a music teacher who could also give some instruction in general subjects."

"A most diabolical plot," I said, feeling glad that I had come.

He chuckled. "With a violinist and a pianist and a singer," he said, "we shall be able to do a great deal."

"A singer?" I inquired.

9

"Oh yes," he said hurriedly. "You will come with us for at least part of the time? Glen Elan would just suit you."

"You are very kind," I said doubtfully. "But let me hear the rest of the plot."

He looked a little worried. "Ah, that is where I wished to ask your advice. The most promising of the applicants says she is not at all sure that she knows enough arithmetic. Do you think arithmetic is very necessary to Vincent?"

"How much does he know already?" I said gravely.

"I do not altogether know," said his father, "but I should think he has probably picked up some."

"He hasn't had any definite lessons?"

"No. I do not think there is anyone who would have given them to him."

"In that case," I pronounced, "she ought to know enough to start him."

He was overjoyed. "To-morrow afternoon she is coming for an interview. I arranged it for when you were here. And I shall simply ask her to play something. If she plays it with soul I shall engage her."

I smiled.

He was silent for a few moments, then he said, "Though there is no harm at all in what I am doing, I should so much prefer it if my wife were not present at the interview. So would you be kind enough to take her into the garden just before three o'clock to-morrow afternoon, and then if the governess can play I will bring her out to you both?"

With vows of the uttermost secrecy I joined in the conspiracy.

After dinner that evening he led me solemnly into the drawing-room. In spite of his passion for music the room had a desolate, unoccupied air, and the music was arranged too neatly. He shut the door very carefully and drew a heavy curtain across it.

"What are you going to sing?" he asked.

I answered that I would try something from *Don Giovanni*.

In delight he picked up from the floor a neat score bound in bright red leather, and, opening it at the beginning of the overture, he put it on the piano and went and sat down in a chair.

"We will sit quietly for a moment and imagine the overture," he said, and he sat and listened to the exquisite inaudible notes. I, of course, could not remember it all through. Afterwards he made me sing until I was hoarse, and though I had not sung for a long time and my voice had never been much to boast about, he seemed to derive such pleasure from it that he would have affected me with his enthusiasm had I not been unpleasantly aware of Mrs Everett somewhere within hearing of this not very sound-proof room.

The next day just before three o'clock I asked Mrs Everett if she would let me take her into the garden. She accepted my escort without any suspicion, and I do not know why I felt so desperately wicked and conscience-stricken. She dragged very heavily on my arm, and we walked only to a seat by the side of a croquet lawn. She hardly spoke, except to admire the yellow roses and the woods in the distance.

She said, "You will like Glen Elan. George says you are coming there with us for some of the time."

"If you are sure that you would like me to come," I said.

"It is quiet, of course," she remarked, without answering, "but if you like walking you can make a good holiday there."

I thanked her again, and promised that I would come there in August.

"Good," she said, and seemed quite pleased.

I was rather glad, too, that I should not visit them entirely on my merits as a singer.

Soon after this Everett came pirouetting across the garden, and with him a quaint little figure who was the music teacher. She was smiling shyly, but with delight, so she had evidently played with soul. He led her up to us.

"This is the lady I have engaged as a governess for Vincent, my dear," he said to his wife. "Her name is Miss Antonia Trenier."

Miss Antonia smiled timidly. She was a small creature, not even as tall as Everett. She had a very high forehead and big black eyes, and she made quick and startled, yet at the same time reposeful, movements. She wore a comical little, loosely knitted striped coat, which reached only to her waist, and looked too small for anyone, and a long, full, white pleated skirt, while a childish little white straw hat on her head proclaimed that she was in the country.

"You will find Vincent quite easy to manage," said Mrs Everett. "He is a docile child."

"Oh yes, thank you," said Antonia, and sat down on the seat next to her.

"This is Mr Elliott," said Mrs Everett. "He is coming to Scotland with us for part of the time."

"Oh yes," said Antonia, giving me a little bow from where she sat.

I found it a little difficult not to show my amusement at this music teacher who had answered Everett's "carefully worded advertisement" and did not know much arithmetic. Everett, of course, sat looking at her as though she were a new piano.

Mrs Everett suggested that she should stay to tea, and sent Everett scurrying off to the house to have it brought out to the garden.

She turned to Antonia. "Why did you apply for the post?" she asked abruptly.

Antonia looked rather frightened. "I had had no holiday for a very long time," she said. "I thought it would be very nice to go to Scotland, although I will have to put off all my pupils to do so."

"What do you teach?" asked Mrs Everett.

"Music," said Antonia, looking surprised.

"Oh," said Mrs Everett. "I used to play once, but now my health is too bad."

Antonia looked rather startled, and evidently did not know what to say.

"Are you very fond of music?" I asked.

"Oh yes," said Antonia. "My father played the violin in an orchestra. He played very well, but he was without ambition."

"And you are not without ambition?" I remarked.

"I do not know," said she. "Teaching is very tiring to the temperament."

"Yes, it must be," I agreed.

Everett came out again and we had tea. Mrs Everett did not speak, and looked across to the woods. Everett was in complete bliss, and Antonia as full of excitement as any child would be before a holiday. Nobody seemed to think of introducing Vincent to his new governess, so when an opportunity presented itself I suggested it. Then Everett ran to fetch him, and returned with the little fellow hurrying after him.

"This is your new governess, Vincent," said his father. "She is coming to Glen Elan with us, and she is going to teach you a great many interesting things."

"Oh yes," said Antonia, bobbing down to his level to shake hands with him. "Music, you know."

Vincent looked at her shyly and said, "Thank you very much."

"But he need not learn music," said Everett.

Antonia looked up at us. "But——" she began.

I broke in hurriedly and a little maliciously with, "Arithmetic and things like that, Miss Trenier."

She looked from Everett, who was looking rather apprehensive, to me, but seeing that I was smiling, she laughed too, and having very little notion what to do with Vincent, she patted him on the shoulder and went back to her seat.

Soon afterwards she went to catch her train. The next day I, too, went back to town, after promising to join them at Glen Elan the first week in August.

On the second day of August I walked up the glen. Right from its foot I could see the house where the Everetts were staying—the roof was just visible above the trees. Everett had called it a cottage, but it looked more imposing than that. Half-way up the glen the road ended at a little lodge built of dark grey stone, and I had to climb over a stile. After this the path led under the trees by the side of a little burn running through the glen. When I reached the house it really was a cottage after all, for it was built high up at the head of the glen, and for that reason, only, overtopped the trees.

They were all very glad to see me. Everett shook my hand with enormous vigour, and Antonia and Vincent greeted me with shy enthusiasm, while the landlord's little girl stared at me from behind Vincent's back in wonder and astonishment. Mrs Everett was not so well, I learnt, but she was in the house and anxious to welcome me, so I went in at once to see her. She was lying propped up with cushions on a sofa by the window, and though she smiled and talked to me, I was quite shocked to see that she looked much worse and that the lines of pain on her face had deepened.

August went quickly. I tramped the whole countryside, sometimes alone, sometimes taking Vincent, though then only for short walks, because I would never have dared offer to carry him. Sometimes, too, Everett came with me, never without a hat and gloves, and he would always chuckle delightedly at my wandering around the country with no hat, as though that were a convincing proof of my musical temperament, though it seemed to me more a proof of the contrary. I spent some of the time, too, in talking to Mrs Everett, partly because no one else did so, and partly because I liked to. But in the evenings we had music: Antonia at the piano; the landlord, a dark, sulky man who played Scots melodies beautifully, and other things by ear haltingly, with his violin at her side. We obeyed Everett like slaves, even to the extent of playing or singing a single phrase a dozen times over, while he, standing on his toes in the middle of the carpet, strung up to a pitch of the most rapturous torment, would drink in the essence of every note.

Antonia played well, but with more of what she would have called temperament than technical excellence. She would begin lightly and timidly, but half-way through, as if the spirit of Everett, swaying, hugging himself, chuckling, and even weeping by her side, had taken possession of her, she would play so that I believe if the house had caught fire she would have gone on playing.

The landlord had an immense respect for Everett, and indeed took no notice of anyone else in the house except his little daughter. If Antonia played anything for him wrongly, he showed towards her the most uncompromising hostility, and waited in silence for Everett to put the matter right. For my part I sang anything Everett asked for, whether I could sing it well or not. It was impossible to sing to him and retain one's self-consciousness; he extracted beauty from the most halting performance, so that one soon learnt simply, as it were, to tell him the words and notes of the song and let him interpret it as he would. We went on like this for a week or so, and then one morning something really rather exciting happened.

Everett and I had started out for a bit of a walk, but before we had gone far some large drops of rain fell and entirely dissuaded him from going. So we turned and went back. As we reached the house we heard the opening bars of a song being played, and then, as we listened, the first long, waving note came out to us in a lovely, low, clear soprano voice. It went on smoothly, flowingly, through a sustained and rather difficult song, and then, suddenly refusing to take some high notes, stopped.

Everett ran into the house and I went after him.

"Don't sing that," he was saying to Antonia; "sing something I like."

Antonia, trembling with apprehension, began to sing the song he found for her, and sang it all through. Her voice was really beautiful, only sometimes at the top notes it sounded as though her throat had closed up with fright at the thought of them. Everett looked down at her in an agony of excitement and said reproachfully :

"You have been here all this time and have never sung for me. Haven't I been kind to you ?"

"Oh yes," she said, putting her hands out towards him.

He took hold of them and knelt down on the floor in front of her.

"Then why ?"

"Because," she said, beginning to cry," I have not been able to have any lessons for a long time, and I thought I couldn't sing now. I used to sing when I was a girl."

"How long ago was it that you were a girl ?" he asked, putting her hand against his cheek.

She smiled a little and said sternly, "I will be a great singer or no singer at all. Don't you think it is wrong to be without ambition ?"

"Sing for me," he said, and his voice trembled with the most excruciating happiness, "and you will give me so much joy that I shall believe that I have been deaf for my whole life up to now."

"Yes, I will," she said solemnly.

Everett got up quickly and hurried out of the room.

After that, of course, we had a wonderful time. Antonia's voice really was beautiful. But whereas before this we had played and sung only what Everett wanted, now Antonia chose to sing whatever she liked, and the influence of her father, the violinist without ambition, began to be felt. And it was very amusing to discover how utterly intolerant Everett was towards any music of a type he did not like, and he had very definite preferences. He would willingly have ignored everything that was not written before Beethoven. Once I remember Antonia singing Mendelssohn's "On Wings of Song" in her smooth, flowing voice, and though he listened politely, and even waited a few seconds before he made her sing some Scarlatti, it was clear that he did not like it, and the next morning at breakfast he attacked Mendelssohn and all that he stands for with intense vigour. And Antonia, turning to me, complained, "But I am so fond of music in which the left hand goes up and down perpetually."

Her voice improved a great deal under Everett's enthusiasm for it. Most of the songs she sang beautifully, but when they came to the high notes she would frown and blush, and the violin would play the bars by itself until she joined in again; and during her little silences she and Everett would exchange the glances of those who pass together through some great suffering. And all this aroused him to such a pitch of excitement that he even insisted on singing himself, in a ridiculous thin whisper of a tenor voice.

Meanwhile my relations with the rest of the household developed. Vincent, who wandered about the glen in idyllic freedom, except for the short time every morning when Antonia gave him lessons, began to make friends with me. He had acquired the borrowing habit, and one morning he walked up to me and said, "Please would you mind lending me your big knife?"

"What for?" I asked.

"Well, the truf is, I want to show it to the little boy down at the lodge, so if you are not using it——"

"All right," I said, handing it over. "Only be careful."

"Yes," he said; then after a minute's hesitation he pointed gallantly to the landlord's little girl, who still stared at me with astonishment and wonder, and said, "Do you think you have anything you could lend Jean too?"

I thought for a moment, and then fished out my beautiful red silk handkerchief and tied it round her curly head. And down the glen they went hand in hand, until the red handkerchief disappeared among the trees. Soon they returned with the good-natured, fat little boy from the lodge half-way down the glen, who used to share Vincent's lessons with Antonia while his father and uncle went out fishing. And Vincent said, "Please could you lend this little boy something to hold just for to-day?"

All I had with me was an old cigar cutter, but the fat little boy received it with reverence. After this the children came to me nearly every morning, and I collected quite a repertoire of possessions which one might borrow. Fortunately, little Jean never wanted anything but the red handkerchief.

Mrs Everett grew daily worse and worse, and the doctor from the village at the foot of the glen would not allow her to get up from bed now. Everett, beyond asking her if she had everything that she wanted, paid not much attention to her, while Antonia never went near her. I used sometimes to take Vincent to see her, but she took very little notice of him, and he simply stood shyly in the doorway until she told him he might go. She always seemed glad to see me, and once she asked me to come again.

Once, too, she sent for me to move her bed nearer to the window. She never mentioned Everett, and only once she asked me if I thought that Antonia had a good voice. I answered that I thought it very good, and then could think of nothing else to say.

She said, "I get very tired of music. I would like to hear some Beethoven again, though, before I die."

"Shall I ask her to play some Beethoven for you?" I said awkwardly.

"No, no, I don't want that," she answered.

They had intended to leave at the end of August, but Mrs Everett was so much worse that the doctor advised them not to risk the journey. When September came she sent for Antonia. I was in the bedroom when she came up. It was the first time she had seen Mrs Everett for days, and she greeted her with a kind of frightened shyness and inattention.

"Miss Trenier," said Mrs Everett, "you have not forgotten that Vincent goes to school in three days' time? I should be very grateful if you would help Ellen to pack for him; you will have more of an idea what he will require. Also, if you are going back to London when you leave here, perhaps you will be kind enough to let him travel with you. We shall not be able to leave yet."

It was very clear that Antonia had forgotten
that the two months had gone. Why, she had
probably forgotten that it was as a governess
that she was there. She darted one startled
glance at us and ran out of the room. Mrs
Everett turned to me and said, "The time goes
very quickly."

In a few moments Everett came running upstairs. He could hardly wait until he was in
the room to ask her, "Do you think it is entirely
necessary for Vincent to go to school at the
beginning of the term?"

"Yes," said his wife. "Don't you think so,
Mr Elliott?"

I hesitated. "I think it would be best," I
said. "You see, he might be home-sick, and it
won't be so bad if there are other new boys too.
It would be much lonelier for him in the middle
of the term. And he will be behind with his
lessons too, because he doesn't know much as
it is. Though, of course, he is sharp enough.
He might get ragged, you know," I ended
weakly.

"Ragged?" said his father.

"Yes, he must go," said Mrs Everett.
"Antonia will travel down with him."

"But wouldn't you want him to stay with
you a little longer?" asked Everett in anguish.
"You might——"

"No, thank you," said Mrs Everett.

After this Antonia and Everett went about with tragedy written on their faces. As we sat at meals they would suddenly look at each other, and tears would come to their eyes and sometimes fall tumbling down their cheeks. For my part I was chiefly concerned about Vincent, though he was as much unconcerned about his coming adventure as the rest of them. I asked him if he wanted to go to school.

"I don't know," he said, looking up at me. "I suppose it will be very nice."

When I tried to tell him from my own recollections what the first term at a boarding school usually is like, he pointed out, with some reason, "But things must be very different now, you know, because it is a long time since you went to school first, and things change quickly."

I suggested to Everett that he should give the little fellow a watch to take to school with him. He was very grateful for the suggestion, and at lunch that day he solemnly handed Vincent his own gold watch.

"Is it for me to borrow?" asked Vincent breathlessly.

"No, you may keep it to take to school," said his father.

Vincent was overwhelmed, but somehow it annoyed me. There was something inappropriate and unfriendly about the gift. I tried to remedy it by sending for a cheap watch for him to use on less solemn occasions. I interviewed Mrs Everett's maid about a tuck-box, but her mind refused to apprehend the concept, so I ordered as good a collection as I could think of to be sent on to his school, without consulting anyone else.

The next morning Antonia went walking down the glen, and I was sitting in Mrs Everett's room when I saw her come hurrying back. A few minutes later Everett came running upstairs, the look of unbearable happiness almost returned to his face.

"Antonia has been asked to stay at the lodge for a short time to go on teaching the little boy there." He paused.

Mrs Everett said nothing.

"But who will take Vincent to school?" I asked rather angrily.

"Oh yes," said Everett, trying to think.

"He can travel in the care of the guard," said his mother.

"Oh yes," said Everett, and scurried downstairs.

"Will someone meet him at the other end?" I asked.

"Yes," she said. "I have already written to them."

"You know, it is time I went," I said. "Would you like me to take him?"

"No," she said quickly. "Don't you go yet. Stay a little longer. He will be all right." She looked at me almost appealingly.

I assured her that I would be glad to stay, only I insisted on being allowed to take him as far as Glasgow and see the guard myself.

Downstairs the tragedy lightened a little until the evening. Then Antonia sang. She sang until Everett stood listening to her with tears rolling down his cheeks, and until she was so excited that she stopped playing and only the violin followed her voice up and down, while her hands, reflected in the wood of the piano, waved and fluttered like its echo.

Then she got up from the piano and went to get her hat, because she was going to the lodge that very night. And I had to take her there because Everett was too much overcome by grief; and, as though not to spoil the memory of the music by hearing any other sounds, they did not say good-bye. He went back into the house, and she took my arm and walked slowly down the glen. And really, when in a few minutes we reached the lodge, the place of her exile seemed ridiculously near, and I lost all patience with them.

The next day I took Vincent to Glasgow and

put him in the train for London. As we waited to go, looking at the little chap sitting there alone, I felt acutely responsible for him, and I said, "Do you collect foreign stamps?"

"No," he said, "up to now I haven't."

"Well, if you would care to write to me," I said casually, "I live in Egypt, you know, and I could easily send you some stamps. If you don't collect them yourself you could swop them with other boys."

"Yes, thank you very much," he said.

"And you could tell me at the same time how you like school, and how you are getting on."

"Yes," he said, and the train began to move. I ran along by the side, and at the last minute impulsively gave him my big knife, although I had had it a long time.

When I got back to the glen Mrs Everett was very much worse. The doctor came up every day, although we were so far from the village, and for a week Everett did not see Antonia, for she would not come to the cottage, and he did not leave it. He spent his time wandering aimlessly about the house, and once I discovered him seated on the piano-stool with some music in front of him, letting his fingers rest silently on the notes. Mrs Everett grew worse every day.

At last, one evening, Everett asked me to walk down to the lodge with him. He hardly spoke on the way there, and I, come straight from talking to his wife, felt too much out of sympathy with him to speak. All that he and Antonia were doing was waiting for her to die, and it certainly would not take long. I caught myself wondering if Antonia watched the doctor every day as he passed the lodge on his way back from the cottage; but then I was angry with myself, because it was a woman very different from Antonia whom I imagined leaning out of the window to gaze intently at his face.

When we reached the lodge we heard her singing the opening bars of Bellini's *Casta Diva* ("in which the left hand goes up and down perpetually"), but she could not sing much of it. She stopped singing, and came through the French window on to the lawn a little above us. Everett called to her, and she came slowly down the bank and clung to the rusty iron railings which separated us.

"I can't sing it," she said mournfully, pulling her handkerchief tight between her hands.

Everett put his hand out and stroked her hair. She squeezed herself through a place where the railings were broken instead of going to the gate, and stood looking up at him.

"You shall have lessons," he said, and put his arms round her and kissed her with the profoundest tenderness, and then he stood with his head thrown back and the look of excruciating joy on his face.

It would have made very little difference to them if I had stayed, so I left them there, and, feeling rather depressed, went back to the cottage.

A few days afterwards Mrs Everett died. I was sitting by her bedside, and I thought she was asleep when she opened her eyes and said, "Don't let me be buried here."

"I hope you will get well," I said; "but I will do whatever you wish."

"It will be a lot of trouble to take me home, but don't let them bury me anywhere near here."

"No," I promised.

"Good," she said, and closed her eyes again, and in less than an hour she was dead.

Everett behaved at her death very much as he had behaved when she was ill. He was vaguely sorry for her, but he did not altogether understand what was expected of him. It was not until we were ready to leave that he seemed to realise that now he could fetch Antonia and take her home. Then he was overjoyed, and the three of us went down in the same train with Mrs Everett's body. I went home with him and helped to make arrangements for the funeral, and Antonia went back to town.

I did not see them again until the evening I

returned to Egypt, and they came to the station to wish me good-bye. They were full of excitement, and told me all their plans for the future. I suppose they got married pretty soon afterwards.

"And when you come to see us again," said Everett, "she will be able to sing everything."

"Yes, everything," said Antonia, beginning to wave her handkerchief to me.

And then they stood waving after the train, and the look of intolerable joy on Everett's face seemed as though it would never go away until he died from the intensity of it.

A COUNTRY HOUSE

From the day when I first met my wife she has been my first consideration always. It is only fair that I should treat her so, because she is young. When I met her she was a mere child, with black ringlets down her back and big blue eyes. She put her hair up to get married. Not that I danced attendance on her. That is nonsense. But from the very first moment I saw her I allowed all those barriers and screens that one puts up against people's curiosity to melt away. Nobody can do more than that. It takes many years to close up all the doors to your soul. And then a woman comes along, and at the first sight of her you push them all open, and you become a child again. Nobody can do more than that.

And then at the first sight of a stranger she begins talking about "community of interests" and all that sort of thing. I must tell you we live in the country, a long way from a town, so we have no electric light. It is a disadvantage, but you must pay something for living in the country. It is a big house, too, and carrying lamps and candles from one end of it to another is hard. Not that it worries me. I have lived here since I was born. I can find my way about in the dark. But it is natural that a woman would not like it.

I had thought about it for a long time. I do not know anything about electrical engineering, but there is a stream running right down the garden; not a very small stream either. Now why not use the water for a little power-station of our own and make our own electricity?

I went up to town and called at the electricians. They would send someone down to look at it. But they could not send anyone until September. Their man was going for his holidays the next day. He would be away until September. Now I suddenly felt that there was a great hurry. I wanted it done before September. They had no one else they could send, and it would take some time if I decided to have it done. I asked them to send for the electrician. I would pay him anything he liked if he would put off his holiday. They sent for him, and he came in and listened to my proposal.

At this point I ought to describe his appearance. He was tall, about forty years old. He had blue eyes, and grey hair brushed straight up. His hair might have been simply fair, not grey. I cannot remember that now. He had almost a military appearance, only he was shy, reserved, and rather prim. His voice was at least an octave deeper than is natural in a speaking voice. He smiled as though he was amused at everyone else's amusement, only this was not contemptuous.

Do not think for a moment that I regard this as a melodrama. I do not. I saw at once that he was a nice fellow, something out of the ordinary, not a villain at all.

He smiled when I asked him to put off his vacation. Nothing could be done until he had had a look at the place, and he was perfectly willing to come down that evening to see it. If it were possible to start work at once, something could perhaps be arranged. I was pleased with this, and I invited him to stay the night with us.

At five o'clock he was standing on the office steps with a very small bag, which he carried as if it were too light for him. He climbed into the car, and sat in silence during the whole long drive. When we reached the avenue of trees just before we turn in at my gate (although it was still twilight, under the trees it was quite dark, because they are so thick), he said, "I should imagine this was very dark at night?"

"Yes, as black as pitch," I said.

"It would be a good thing to have a light here. It looks dangerous."

"No, I don't want one here," I said. "Nobody uses this road at night but I, and I know it in the dark. Light in the house will be enough."

I wonder if he thought that unreasonable or

not. He was silent again. We turned in at the gate. My wife came across the lawn to meet us. I do not know how to describe her. That day she had a large white panama hat and a dress with flowers on it. I said before that she had black hair and blue eyes. She is tall, too, and she still looks very young. The electrician —his name was Richardson—stood with his feet close together and bowed from the waist. I told her that I had brought him here to see if it was possible to put in electric light.

"In the house?" she said. "That would be lovely. Is it possible at all?"

"I hope so," said Richardson in his deep voice. I could see that she was surprised at it.

"We don't know yet," I said; "we must take him to see the stream."

She came with us. The stream runs down by the side of the house, curving a little with the slope of the garden, until it joins the larger stream which flows between the garden wall and the fields. We followed it down, not going round by the paths, but jumping over flower-beds and lawns. Richardson looked all the time at the water, except once when he helped my wife across a border.

"There is enough water," he said, "and I suppose it is fuller than this sometimes?"

"Yes, when it rains," said my wife. "Sometimes it is impossible to cross the stepping-stones without getting one's shoes wet."

Now I will tell you where the stepping-stones are. Where the stream curves most a wide gravelled path crosses it, and some high stones have been put in the water. When we came down as far as that Richardson said, "This is the place where we could have it. We could put a small engine-house here, and the water could afterwards be carried through pipes to join the stream down below, forming a sort of triangle with the hypotenuse underground."

I asked him if he was certain that it could be done.

"I think so," he said seriously.

My wife smiled at him. "I hope the building will not be ugly; it would spoil the garden."

Richardson smiled in the amused way and answered, "It will, but it will not be high. We must have it at least half underground, with steps to go down to it. Would it be possible to plant some thick trees round it? Yews, so long as they do not interfere with the wires."

"Oh yes, thank you," she said. "I believe we could have that."

Richardson looked about him a bit more, and he took some measurements with a tape-measure from his pocket. Then we went back to the house. At dinner I asked him where he meant to spend his holiday.

"I am not sure," he said seriously. "I thought perhaps the Yorkshire moors would be a good place."

"You won't find anything better than this," I said. "Put off your holiday until September."

My wife moved to the door. "Would you have to stay here during the work?" she asked.

"Or somewhere near here, madam," he said.

"Yes, of course, here," she said, and walked out of the room. Richardson bowed from the waist again.

We arranged it easily. He would not put it off, but he would make this his holiday. He would bring his motor bike here and explore the country around. He could be here always when there was anything for him to do, and he considered our invitation to him to stay here more than enough compensation for the change of his plans.

Afterwards in the drawing-room he asked my wife if she was fond of music.

"That is what she *is* fond of," I said. "She plays the piano."

What can anyone do with a strange man in the drawing-room but play the piano to him? She played a Chopin nocturne. Now I could watch girls dancing to Chopin's music all day,

but to play Chopin to a stranger that you meet
for the first time! What must he think of you?
I can understand her playing even the nocturnes
when she is alone. When one is alone one is in
the mood for anything. But to choose to play
them when she is meeting someone for the first
time! That is simply wrong. Chopin's nights
are like days. There is no difference, except that
they are rounded off. That is nonsense. Night
does not round things off. Night is a distorter.
These nocturnes come of never having spent his
nights alone, of spending them either in an inn
or in someone else's bedroom. No! How do I
know what Chopin did? But I tell you they are
the result of thinking of darkness as the absence
of the sun's light. It is better to think of it as
a vapour rising from the depths of the earth and
perhaps bringing many things with it.

But he liked it. That is, Richardson liked the
nocturne. He asked her to play another. While
she turned over the pages I said aloud, "Night
isn't like that. Night is a distorter."

My wife looked into the darkness outside the
window.

Richardson looked at her, then he looked at
me in uncertainty. She began to play, and he,
for a moment pretending to be apologetic, studied
her music with concentration.

Why didn't they ask me what I meant? I

could have proved it to them. In any case it was an interesting point.

She played a lot of Chopin. Then as she came from the piano she said, "You are fond of music too. Do you play?"

"No," he said. "It was my great ambition to be a 'cellist, but I never learnt to play it well, and I haven't one now. It is my favourite instrument."

"It is only the heavy father of a violin," I said. But I said it only because all that Chopin had annoyed me. I like the 'cello very much.

"I have never liked anything better than the piano," said my wife. "I am sorry you do not play."

"He sings," I said.

He smiled with amusement.

"Do you?" she asked eagerly.

"Yes," he said, half bowing from where he sat.

"I knew by your speaking voice," I said. "Please let us hear you."

"I will bring some songs with me if you wish it," he said. "That is very kind of you," and he leaned back in his chair and cut off all communication with us.

We sat in silence until my wife left us. Then we talked a little about the electric light and then went to bed.

The next day .the work began. Until the small building was up and the pipes laid from it back to the stream, Richardson could do nothing more than see that the measurements were right. He carried a small black notebook, and kept looking at it and then looking up at us and saying, "This is no work at all, you know; it is simply like a holiday."

He brought his motor bike down, but he went for few rides. Most of the time he spent looking at the first few bricks of the building, or crossing and recrossing the stream over the stepping-stones, with no hat on, and his black notebook open in one hand, as though he were making some very serious calculations. I do not suppose he was for a moment.

As I said before, I do not regard this as a melodrama. I do not consider him a villain, but, on the contrary, a nice enough fellow, but it was irritating to me the way he wandered round in a circle looking for something to do.

In the daytime he could look after himself, but in the evening we treated him as a guest.

The second day he was here, after tea I suggested taking him for a walk. He bowed with one hand behind his back, and he kept it there afterwards. I noticed it particularly. My wife came too. We walked down the garden. Richardson, still with his hand behind his back, walking just behind her, talked to her about the work, and he said the same things over twice.

When we got to the bottom of the garden and through the door which opens on the bank of the stream she gave a cry of horror. And I will tell you why. It was because I had had the grass and weeds on the banks cut.

She turned to Richardson. "I am so sorry," she said. "You should have seen this before it was cut. It was very pretty. What were those white flowers growing on the other side?"

"Hemlock," I said. "It had to be cut."

"I don't see why," she said. "It is a pity to spoil such a beautiful place for the sake of tidiness." She turned to him petulantly.

Now that is all nonsense. A place must be tidy. There were bulrushes and water-lilies as it was. What more must she have? A lot of weeds dripping down into the water! There is a difference between garden flowers and weeds. If you want weeds, then do not have gardens. And I suppose I am insensible to beauty because I keep the place cut and trimmed. Nonsense! Suppose my wife took off her clothes and ran about the garden like a bacchante! Perhaps I should like it very much, but I should shut her up in her room all the same.

We walked along in silence over the newly cut grass. It was yellow already with having been

left uncut too long. I went first across the
bridge, and my two friends who admire Chopin
so much came after. We were in the cornfield
now, and I will tell you what it is like. There
is a little hill just opposite the bridge, and the
corn grows on top of it and on its slopes. It is
a very small hill, but the country around is flat,
and from the top of it you can see over the trees
a long distance. We began to walk up the path
to the top. The corn was cut and stood up in
sheaves. That is what I like.

When we reached the top Richardson took his
hand from behind his back and looked around
him. There is a lake a few miles away, and on
either side of it the land rises and there are trees.
Beyond that again is the sea. And from the hill
the sea looks nearer than it is and the lake like
a bay. Richardson thought it was a bay. I
thought so too when I was a child.

"I did not know the sea was so near," he
said.

"It isn't near," I answered. "That is a lake.
There are even houses in between it and the sea,
only you cannot see them."

He took a deep breath. "You know, it is
very kind of you to let me stay here. It is very
beautiful. I have not seen a place I like better.
I am most grateful. And the work is simply
nothing. It is a real holiday." At this point

he fingered the black notebook which stuck out of his pocket.

If things had not happened as they did he might have come down often; he might have spent his week-ends here. He was not a bad sort of fellow.

He did not want to leave the hill, but my wife did not like walking about on the stubble in her thin shoes. We walked back by the path which leads between a low wall and some small fir-trees to the back of the house. I had the path made for her, because she prefers that walk.

After dinner Richardson sang. His voice was all right, deep like his speaking voice, only not so steady. She played for him, and he stood up at attention, except that, with his right arm bent stiffly at the elbow and pressed to his side, he clutched the lapel of his coat. He sang some Brahms. It was quite nice.

I went to write some letters, and afterwards I walked about in the garden. When I returned they had left the piano and were talking. He was very fond of Strauss. She had not heard the *Alpine* symphony. We were so far from everywhere here.

The time went on. Richardson grew more restless every day. And yet he was lethargic too. He hardly left the house and garden, and he still wandered back and forth by the work.

He did not interfere with the men by giving unnecessary orders, but he still studied his notebook as though there were important calculations there. I know all this, because I watched him as if he were my brother.

My wife used to go down there to sit sometimes in the mornings. But he hardly spoke to her then. It is natural that a man would not care to talk about music and all that when the men were working in the sun. It was curious how much interest we all took in the little building and the pipes and the water, and yet when we thought of the electric light in the house, which was to be the result, all the romance was gone out of it. This is not simply my experience. It was so with my wife and Richardson too. I know by my own observation of them. The minute the building was finished we went down to see it. Nothing but a yellow brick hut with steps to go down, and an opening like the mouth of a letter-box in the wall nearest the stream.

"The water is shut off now," said Richardson. "We have to put a grating in it before the water comes through."

There was a hole in the concrete floor too, and from that the pipes would lead back to the stream. The first pipe was there with a big curve in it. It was nice to see it getting on. After that they

dug a ditch and put the pipes down. He helped
them to dig.

Every night he sang and my wife played, but
I did not always stay in the drawing-room. One
night, though, I remember particularly, he sang
a song by Hugo Wolf about a girl whose lover
had gone, and while the men and women were
binding the corn she went to the top of a hill,
and the wind played with the ribbon that he had
put in her hat. It was something like that; I
have forgotten it. I asked him to sing it again.
I suppose they were pleased that I liked something. He sang it.

" An dem Hut mein Rosenband, von seiner Hand
    Spielet in dem Winde."

Now I should think that the hill that she
climbed in that song was like the hill in our
cornfield, and the girl sat there for hours "like
one lost in a dream."

The days passed, and everything remained the
same except the work, and that went on quickly.
We walked about together sometimes. One
evening we went again through the door to
the little river where the grass had been cut.
We were going along the bank talking when we
heard a splash, and there was a boy swimming
in the water. I shouted to him, and told him
to come out and not swim there again. His

white back flashed through the water to a bush on the other side, and he began to dress behind it. When I turned back she said, "Why did you send him away? It looked so nice."

"He can go somewhere else to swim," I said. Richardson said nothing.

"He does no harm here, surely?" she said.

Bulrushes and water-lilies are not enough for her. She must have weeds and naked boys too. And do you think *she* ever bathed in a river when she was a child, and hid behind a bush when someone was coming? No, of course not. And does she think the boy wants to be seen bathing? And if he is not to be seen when he is here, he might as well go somewhere else.

We never talked about anything except the work, and he talked about music with my wife. They never said anything illuminating on the subject, though. It is a funny thing that you can spend days and weeks with a man and never mention anything but water-pipes and electricity. But, after all, you can't talk about God and Immortality to a man you hardly know. Anyhow, it is nice to see someone so much interested in his work. No. That is nonsense. He was not interested in his work. When the engine came we were enthusiastic, and he was as miserable as sin. What business has an electrician to get excited over yellow bricks and water-pipes? He was restless. He could not settle to anything. If he read a book, half the time it would be open on his knee and he looking away from it. I noticed him very particularly.

The day before everything was finished and he was to go—he was not waiting to see the light actually put in the rooms—I was chalking out a garden-bed just at the bottom of the garden by the door. It is a shady place, and I meant to plant violets there, especially white violets— not in August, of course, but it was better to get it prepared while I thought of it. I heard them coming along on the other side of the wall.

She was saying, "Before I was married I stayed with my music master in London. He had two sons but no daughters. His wife was very fond of me. That was the happiest time of my life. One of the sons is a first violin now. I went to a symphony concert when we were in London once and saw him play. I don't know what happened to the other one."

"Let us sit down here," said Richardson.

I knew there was something wrong with him by his voice. I detected that at once.

I suppose they sat down on the large tree-stump outside. They were silent for a moment. I suppose she was looking at the water and he was looking at her.

Then he said, beginning as though he were
talking to himself, and yet apologising too,
"Please forgive me, I ought not to say it. I
have never been to a place which has given
me such pleasure as this. I have never noticed
scenery or nature much before. When one likes
a place, it is because one went to it in childhood
or something of that sort. But this has been
so very beautiful while I have been here. I
suppose from the beginning I knew I could not
come here again. It is impossible. Forgive me
saying so." His voice became deeper as he went
on, I noticed that.

"Oh, but you must come here again," she said
anxiously. "There is no one here at all, and
we have so many tastes in common."

"No," he said; "you think I don't mean it.
I walked up and down in the garden just now
and I came to a decision. At first I thought I
would not speak a word to you, but afterwards
I decided it would not make any great difference
if I did. People do not change their lives suddenly. That is, they don't except in literature.
And now I feel at peace about it. No harm at
all—none. I do not mean that literature is
artificial, you know, only that it is concerned
with different people."

Now what word had he spoken that a husband
could not listen to? And yet we would have

looked very interesting from an aeroplane or from a window in heaven.

And do you suppose she wanted to know what he was talking about?

All she said was, "Oh, but my husband has asked you to come here himself. You must come often, and bring your songs. There is no one here to talk about music to. And I cannot go to any concerts, we are so far from every-where."

He was silent. They stood up, and I waited for them to come through the door. I suppose nobody could expect me to hide behind a tree so as to cause them no embarrassment. "Excuse me, I was just passing at this moment. Please go on with your pleasant conversation." However, they chose to go back by the other way along the bank of the stream.

We spent dinner very pleasantly. Nobody spoke a word. Richardson was not fully aware that we were in the room. He looked at the tablecloth. I did not go away to write letters after dinner. I never left the drawing-room. I suppose no one could expect me to do that. After the music we sat round the empty grate and said nothing, and we went very late to bed.

The next morning, after breakfast, I went up to the flagstaff. If you climb up the steep bank at the left of the house and walk along until you

come to a narrow path with trees growing there,
you come to a ledge, and the flagstaff has been
put there, because it can be seen above the trees.
I was standing there disentangling the rope to
pull the flag up when he came up to me.

"What time are you going?" I asked, and
pulled out my watch.

"At eleven," he said.

"I suppose you think it funny that I should
be putting the flag up on the day that you
go?"

"I did not know you had a flagstaff," he said.
"I suppose it can be seen even from the sea?"

"Yes."

He was silent, and he looked across at the
house.

"Where is my wife?" I asked.

"In the drawing-room, practising."

"I hope you will send in your bill as soon as
possible."

"Oh yes," he said. "It will come from the
firm, you know. They pay me. I wanted to
walk round the cornfield before I go."

I pulled up the flag and fastened the cord.
"I'll come with you," I said.

We walked in silence to the top of the hill,
and he stood and looked all round, at the house
and at the sea. Taking leave of it, of course.

"In the village down there," I said, "there is

a very nice girl called Agnes. She isn't pretty, but she is very nice."

Now Agnes was the name of the girl in the song by Hugo Wolf, but I knew he would not see that. He looked at me in surprise. Then he took out his watch and said he must go. There was no need for that. If you go away on a motor bike why go exactly at eleven? He had to keep himself to a time, that is what it was. We turned to go down the hill.

"I put up the flag because it is my birthday," I said, though that was not true.

He looked at me without listening to what I said.

When we got back to the house his motor bike was standing outside the gate ready. He went into the house to fetch his cap, and my wife came out with him. Half-way to the gate he turned to her and thanked her. He had never experienced such pleasure in a holiday before. Then he shook hands with me and said nothing.

"Come down to see us often," I said. "Come whenever you like, for week-ends."

"Oh yes," said my wife, "please come, and bring your music."

He looked embarrassed. I was watching him. I knew he would be. He looked at the ground and mumbled, "Thank you very much. Good-bye." Then he turned and went out through the gate, and in a few minutes he drove away under the trees.

She went into the house. She thinks he will come again, call, and listen to her playing Chopin.

I went to sit down by the engine-house. The engine was working, and it throbbed noisily, while there was hardly any water in the curve of the stream. It has made a great difference to the garden. Up above the flag waved senselessly in the wind.

THE CONQUERED

Last summer, just before my proper holiday, I went to stay with an aunt who lives on the borders of Wales, where there are so many orchards. I must say I went there simply as a duty, because I used to stay a lot with her when I was a boy, and she was, in those days, very good to me. However, I took plenty of books down so that it should not be waste of time.

Of course, when I got there it was really not so bad. They made a great fuss of me. My aunt was as tolerant as she used to be in the old days, leaving me to do exactly as I liked. My cousin Jessica, who is just my age, had hardly changed at all, though they both looked different with their hair up; but my younger cousin Ruth, who used to be very lively and something of a tomboy, had altered quite a lot. She had become very quiet; at least, on the day I arrived she was lively enough, and talked about the fun we used to have there, but afterwards she became more quiet every day, or perhaps it was that I noticed it more. She remembered far more about what we used to do than I did; but I suppose that is only natural, since she had been there all the time in between, and I do not suppose anything very exciting had happened to her, whereas I have been nearly everywhere.

But what I wanted to say is, that not far from my aunt's house, on the top of a little slope, on which there was an apple orchard, was a house with French windows and a large green lawn in front, and in this lived a very charming Welsh lady whom my cousins knew. Her grandfather had the house built, and it was his own design. It is said that he had been quite a friend of the Prince Consort, who once, I believe, actually stayed there for a night.

I knew the house very well, but I had never met any of the family, because they had not always occupied it, and, in any case, they would have been away at the times that I went to my aunt for holidays. Now only this one grand-daughter was left of the family; her father and mother were dead, and she had just come back to live there. I found out all this at breakfast the morning after I came, when Jessica said, "Ruthie, we must take Frederick to see Gwyneth."

"Oh yes," said Ruthie. "Let's go to-day."

"And who is Gwyneth?"

Jessica laughed. "You will be most impressed. Won't he, mother?"

"Yes," said my aunt, categorically.

However, we did not call on her that after-noon, because it poured with rain all day, and it did not seem worth while, though Ruthie

appeared in her macintosh and goloshes ready
to go, and Jessica and I had some difficulty in
dissuading her.

I did not think it was necessary to do
any reading the first day, so I just sat and
talked to the girls, and after tea Jessica and I
even played duets on the piano, which had not
been tuned lately, while Ruthie turned over the
pages.

The next morning, though the grass was wet
and every movement of the trees sent down a
shower of rain, the sun began to shine brightly
through the clouds. I should certainly have
been taken to see their wonderful friend in the
afternoon, only she herself called in the morning.
I was sitting at one end of the dining-room,
reading Tourguéniev with a dictionary and
about three grammars, and I dare say I looked
very busy. I do not know where my aunt was
when she came, and the girls were upstairs. I
heard a most beautiful voice, that was very high-
pitched though, not low, say:

"All right, I will wait for them in here,"
and she came into the room. Of course I had
expected her to be nice, because my cousins liked
her so much, but still they do not meet many
people down there, and I thought they would be
impressed with the sort of person I would he
quite used to. But she really was charming.

She was not very young—older, I should say, than Jessica She was very tall, and she had very fair hair. But the chief thing about her was her finely carved features, which gave to her face the coolness of stone and a certain appearance of immobility, though she laughed very often and talked a lot. When she laughed she raised her chin a little, and looked down her nose in a bantering way. And she had a really perfect nose. If I had been a sculptor I should have put it on every one of my statues. When she saw me she laughed and said, "Ah! I am disturbing you," and she sat down, smiling to herself.

I did not have time to say anything to her before my cousins came in. She kissed Jessica and Ruthie, and kept Ruthie by her side.

"This is our cousin Frederick," said Jessica.

"We have told you about him," said Ruthie gravely.

Gwyneth laughed. "Oh, I recognised him, but how could I interrupt so busy a person! Let me tell you what I have come for. Will you come to tea to-morrow and bring Mr Trenier?" She laughed at me again.

We thanked her, and then my aunt came in.

"How do you do, Gwyneth?" she said. "Will you stay to lunch?"

"No, thank you so much, Mrs Haslett," she

answered. "I only came to ask Jessica and Ruthie to tea to-morrow, and, of course, to see your wonderful nephew. You will come too, won't you?"

"Yes, thank you," said my aunt. "You and Frederick ought to find many things to talk about together."

Gwyneth looked at me and laughed.

Ruthie went out to make some coffee, and afterwards Gwyneth sat in the window-seat drinking it and talking.

"What were you working at so busily when I came in?" she asked me.

"I was only trying to read Tourguéniev in the original," I said.

"Do you like Tourguéniev very much?" she asked, laughing.

"Yes," I said. "Do you?"

"Oh, I have only read one, *Fumée*."

She stayed for about an hour, laughing and talking all the time. I really found her very charming. She was like a personification, in a restrained manner, of Gaiety. Yes, really, very much like Milton's *L'Allegro*.

The moment she was gone Jessica said excitedly, "Now, Frederick, weren't you impressed?"

And Ruthie looked at me anxiously until I answered, "Yes, I really think I was."

57

RHAPSODY

The next day we went there to tea.   It was a beautiful warm day, and we took the short cut across the fields and down a road now overgrown with grass to the bottom of the little slope on which her house was built.   There is an old Roman road not far from here, and I am not quite sure whether that road is not part of it.   We did not go into the house, but were taken at once to the orchard at the back, where she was sitting near a table, and we all sat down with her.   The orchard was not very big, and, of course, the trees were no longer in flower, but the fruit on them was just beginning to grow and look like tiny apples and pears. At the other end some white chickens strutted about in the sunlight.   We had tea outside.

She talked a lot, but I cannot remember now what she said; when she spoke to me it was nearly always to tell me about her grandfather, and the interesting people who used to come to visit him.

When it began to get cool we went into the house across the flat green lawn and through the French window.   We went to a charming room; on the wall above the piano were some Japanese prints on silk, which were really beautiful.   Outside it was just beginning to get dark.

She sang to us in a very nice high soprano

voice, and she chose always gay, light songs which suited her excellently. She sang that song of Schumann, *Der Nussbaum*; but then it is possible to sing that lightly and happily, though it is more often sung with a trace of sadness in it. Jessica played for her. She is a rather good accompanist. I never could accompany singers. But I played afterwards; I played some Schumann too.

"Has Ruthie told you I am teaching her to sing?" said Gwyneth. "I don't know much about it, and her voice is not like mine, but I remember more or less what my master taught me."

"No," I said, looking at Ruthie. "Sing for us now and let me hear."

"No," said Ruthie, and blushed a little. She never used to be shy.

Gwyneth pulled Ruthie towards her. "Now do sing. The fact is you are ashamed of your teacher."

"No," said Ruthie; "only you know I can't sing your songs."

Gwyneth laughed. "You would hardly believe what a melancholy little creature she is. She won't sing anything that is not tearful."

"But surely," I said, "in the whole of Schubert and Schumann you can find something sad enough for you?"

59

"No," said Ruthie, looking at the carpet, "I
don't know any Schumann, and Schubert is
never sad even in the sad songs. Really I can't
sing what Gwyneth sings."

"Then you won't?" I said, feeling rather
annoyed with her.

"No," she said, flushing, and she looked out of
the window.

Ruthie and Jessica are quite different. Jessica
is, of course, like her mother, but Ruthie is like
her father, whom I never knew very well.

Next morning, immediately after breakfast, I
went for a walk by myself, and though I went
by a very roundabout way, I soon found myself
near Gwyneth's house, and perhaps that was not
very surprising. I came out by a large bush of
traveller's-nightshade. I believe that is its name.
At least it is called old man's beard too, but
that does not describe it when it is in flower
at all. You know that it has tiny white waxen
flowers, of which the buds look quite different
from the open flower, so that it looks as though
there are two different kinds of flowers on one
stem. But what I wanted to say was, I came
out by this bush, and there, below me, was the
grass-covered road, with new cart-wheel ruts in
it, which made two brown lines along the green
where the earth showed. Naturally I walked
down it, and stood by the fence of the orchard

below her house. I looked up between the trees, and there she was coming down towards me.

"Good-morning, Mr Trenier," she said, laughing. "Why are you deserting Tourguéniev?"

"It is such a lovely morning," I said, opening the gate for her; "and if I had known I should meet you, I should have felt even less hesitation."

She laughed, and we walked slowly across the grass, which was still wet with dew. It was a perfectly lovely day, with a soft pale blue sky and little white clouds in it, and the grass was wet enough to be bright green.

"Oh, look!" she said suddenly, and pointed to two enormous mushrooms, like dinner-plates, growing at our feet.

"Do you want them?" I asked, stooping to pick them.

"Oh yes," she said; "when they are as big as that they make excellent sauces. Fancy such monsters growing in a night! They were not here yesterday."

"And last week I had not met you," I said, smiling.

She laughed, and took the mushrooms from me.

"Now we must take them to the cook," she said, "and then you shall come for a little walk with me."

As we crossed the lawn to the house she

was carrying the pink-lined mushrooms by their little stalks.

"They look like the sunshades of Victorian ladies," I said.

She laughed, and said, "Did you know that Jenny Lind came here once?"

Afterwards we walked along the real Roman road, now only a pathway with grass growing up between the stones, and tall trees over-shadowing it. On the right is a hill where the ancient Britons made a great stand against the Romans, and were defeated.

"Did you know this was a Roman road?" she asked. "Just think of the charming Romans who must have walked here! And I expect they developed a taste for apples. Does it shock you to know that I like the Romans better than the Greeks?"

I said "No," but now, when I think of it, I believe I *was* a little shocked, although, when I think of the Romans as the Silver Age, I see that silver was more appropriate to her than gold.

She was really very beautiful, and it was a great pleasure to be with her, because she walked in such a lovely way. She moved quickly, but she somehow preserved that same immobility which, though she laughed and smiled so often, made her face cool like stone, and calm.

After this we went for many walks and picnics.

Sometimes the girls came too, but sometimes we went together. We climbed the old battle hill, and she stood at the top looking all around at the orchards on the plain below.

I had meant to stay only a week, but I decided to stay a little longer, or, rather, I stayed on without thinking about it at all. I had not told my aunt and the girls that I was going at the end of the week, so it did not make any difference, and I knew they would expect me to stay longer. The only difference it made was to my holiday, and, after all, I was going for the holiday to enjoy myself, and I could not have been happier than I was there.

I remember how one night I went out by myself down in the direction of her house, where my steps always seemed to take me. When I reached the traveller's-nightshade it was growing dark. For a moment I looked towards her house and a flood of joy came into my soul, and I began to think how strange it was that, although I have met so many interesting people, I should come there simply by chance and meet her. I walked towards the entrance of a little wood, and, full of a profound joy and happiness, I walked in between the trees. I stayed there for a long time imagining her coming gaily into the wood where the moonlight shone through the branches. And I remember thinking suddenly how we have

grown used to believing night to be a sad and
melancholy time, not romantic and exciting as
it used to be. I kept longing for some miracle
to bring her there to me, but she did not come,
and I had to go home.

Then, one evening, we all went to her house
for music and conversation. On the way there
Ruthie came round to my side and said, "Frederick, I have brought with me a song that I can
sing, and I will sing this time if you want me to."

"Yes, I certainly want you to," I said, walking
on with her. "I want to see how she teaches."

"Yes," said Ruthie. "You do see that I could
not sing her songs, don't you?"

In the old days Ruthie and I used to get on
very well, better than I got on with Jessica, who
was inclined to keep us in order then, and I must
say it was very difficult for her to do so.

When we got there, right at the beginning of
the evening Gwyneth sang a little Welsh song.
And I felt suddenly disappointed. I always
thought that the Welsh were melancholy in their
music, but if she sang it sadly at all, it was with
the gossipy sadness of the tea after a funeral.
However, afterwards we talked, and I forgot the
momentary impression.

During the evening Ruthie sang. She sang
Brahms' *An die Nachtigall*, which was really very
foolish of her, because I am sure it is not an easy

thing to sing, with its melting softness and its sudden cries of ecstasy and despair. Her voice was very unsteady, of a deeper tone than Gwyneth's, and sometimes it became quite hoarse from nervousness.

Gwyneth drew her down to the sofa beside her. She laughed, "I told you nothing was sad enough for her."

Ruthie was quite pale from the ordeal of singing before us.

"It is rather difficult, isn't it?" I said.

"Yes," said Ruthie, flushing.

"Have you ever heard a nightingale?" asked Gwyneth of me.

"No," I said.

"Why, there is one in the wood across here; I have heard it myself," said Jessica. "On just such a night as this," she added, laughing, and looking out of the window at the darkness coming to lie on the tops of the apple trees beyond the green lawn.

"Ah! you must hear a nightingale as well as read Tourguéniev, you know," said Gwyneth.

I laughed.

But later on in the evening I was sitting near the piano looking over a pile of music by my side. Suddenly I came across Chopin's *Polnische Lieder*. It is not often that one finds them. I looked up in excitement and said, "Oh, do you

65

know the *Polens Grabgesang*? I implore you to
sing it."

She laughed a little at my excitement and said,
"Yes, I know it. But I can't sing it. It does
not suit me at all. Mrs Haslett, your nephew
actually wants me to sing a funeral march!"

"Oh, please do sing it!" I said. "I have only
heard it once before in my life. Nobody ever
sings it. I have been longing to hear it again."

"It does not belong to me, you know," she
said. "I found it here; it must have belonged
to my father." She smiled at me over the edge
of some music she was putting on the piano.
"No, I can't sing it. That is really decisive."

I was so much excited about the song, because
I shall never forget the occasion on which I first
heard it. I have a great friend, a very wonderful
man, a perfect genius, in fact, and a very strong
personality, and we have evenings at his house,
and we talk about nearly everything, and have
music too, sometimes. Often, when I used to
go, there was a woman there, who never spoke
much but always sat near my friend. She was
not particularly beautiful and had a rather unhappy face, but one evening my friend turned
to her suddenly and put his hand on her shoulder
and said, "Sing for us."

She obeyed without a word. Everybody obeys
him at once. And she sang this song. I shall

never forget all the sorrow and pity for the sorrows of Poland that she put into it. And the song, too, is wonderful. I do not think I have ever heard in my life anything so terribly moving as the part, "O Polen, mein Polen," which is repeated several times. Everyone in the room was stirred, and, after she had sung it, we talked about nothing but politics and the Revolution for the whole of the evening. I do not think she was Polish either. After a few more times she did not come to the evenings any more, and I have never had the opportunity of asking him about her. And although, as I said, she was not beautiful, when I looked at Gwyneth again it seemed to me that some of her beauty had gone, and I thought to myself quite angrily, "No, of course she could not sing that song. She would have been on the side of the conquerors!"

And I felt like this all the evening until we began to walk home. Before we had gone far Jessica said, "Wouldn't you like to stay and listen for the nightingale, Frederick? We can find our way home without you."

"Yes," I said. "Where can I hear her?"

"The best place," said Jessica, "is to sit on the fallen tree—that is where I heard it. Go into the wood by the wild-rose bush with pink roses on it. Do you know it?"

"Yes."

"Don't be very late," said my aunt.

"No," I answered, and left them.

I went into the little wood and sat down on the fallen tree looking up and waiting, but there was no sound. I felt that there was nothing I wanted so much as to hear her sad notes. I remember thinking how Nietzsche said that Brahms' melancholy was the melancholy of impotence, not of power, and I remember feeling that there was much truth in it when I thought of his *Nachtigall* and then of Keats. And I sat and waited for the song that came to

" . . . the sad heart of Ruth, when, sick for home,
She stood in tears amid the alien corn."

Suddenly I heard a sound, and, looking round, I saw Gwyneth coming through the trees. She caught sight of me and laughed.

"You are here too," she said. "I came to hear Jessica's nightingale."

"So did I," I said; "but I do not think she will sing to-night."

"It is a beautiful night," she said. "Anybody should want to sing on such a lovely night."

I took her back to her gate, and I said goodnight and closed the gate behind her. But, all the same, I shall remember always how beautiful she looked standing under the apple trees by the gate in the moonlight, her smile resting like the reflection of light on her carved face. Then, however, I walked home, feeling angry and annoyed with her; but of course that was foolish. Because it seems to me now that the world is made up of gay people and sad people, and however charming and beautiful the gay people are, their souls can never really meet the souls of those who are born for suffering and melancholy, simply because they are made in a different mould. Of course I see that this is a sort of dualism, but still it seems to me to be the truth, and I believe my friend, of whom I spoke, is a dualist, too, in some things.

I did not stay more than a day or two after this, though my aunt and the girls begged me to do so. I did not see Gwyneth again, only something took place which was a little ridiculous in the circumstances.

The evening before I went Ruthie came and said, half in an anxious whisper, "Frederick, will you do something very important for me?"

"Yes, if I can," I said. "What is it?"

"Well, it is Gwyneth's birthday to-morrow, and she is so rich it is hard to think of something to give her."

"Yes," I said, without much interest.

"But do you know what I thought of? I have bought an almond tree—the man has just left it out in the shed—and I am going to plant it at

the edge of the lawn so that she will see it
to-morrow morning. So it will have to be
planted in the middle of the night, and I wondered if you would come and help me."

"But is it the right time of the year to plant
an almond tree—in August?"

"I don't know," said Ruthie; "but surely the
man in the nursery would have said if it were
not. You can sleep in the train, you know.
You used always to do things with me."

"All right, I will," I said, "only we need not
go in the middle of the night—early in the morning will do, before it is quite light."

"Oh, thank you so much," said Ruthie,
trembling with gratitude and excitement. "But
don't tell anyone, will you—not even Jessica?"

"No," I said.

Exceedingly early in the morning, long before
it was light, Ruthie came into my room in her
dressing-gown to wake me, looking exactly as
she used to do. We went quietly downstairs
and through the wet grass to Gwyneth's house,
Ruthie carrying the spade and I the tree. It was
still rather dark when we reached there, but
Ruthie had planned the exact place before.

We hurried with the work. I did the digging,
and Ruthie stood with the tree in her hand looking up at the house. We hardly spoke.

Ruthie whispered, "We must be quiet. That

is her window.   She will be able to see it as soon
as she looks out.   She is asleep now."

"Look here," I said, "don't tell her that I
planted it, because it may not grow.   I can't
see very well."

"Oh, but she must never know that either of
us did it."

"But are you going to give her a present and
never let her know who it is from?"

"Yes," said Ruthie.

"I think that is rather silly," I said.

Ruthie turned away.

We put the tree in.   I have never heard
whether it grew or not.   Just as the sun was
rising we walked back, and that morning I went
away.

TREACHERY IN A FOREST

Mr Wendover, a gentleman with small and wistful blue eyes, and a grey moustache that drooped down on either side of his mouth like the horns of a cow, always spent his summer holiday in a little cottage in the middle of Shelgrove Forest. The cottage was very small and rather broken down, built in the shade of an old and tall tree, and it would have been very much like those cottages in the fairy tales of Hans Andersen, but that it was situated on the main road through the forest, along which motor-cars and motor-buses passed all day, so that even the chickens were covered with dust.

As you know, Shelgrove Forest has become very popular as a centre for motorists, and there is a magnificent new golf-course there and a large hotel. But Mr Wendover always spent the holiday simply in walking about and looking at the trees.

One summer, a few days after his holiday began, he went in the afternoon for a walk to where there is a clearing in the forest, and the trees, which with their tall upright trunks and their crowns of foliage on every branch look like great warrior poets who have received chaplets for victory in all the categories of poetry, give way to land which is comparatively barren, though there are a great many rabbits on it. Mr Wendover sat down here, and put his panama hat by his side and looked at the trees.

Before he had been there very long he heard footsteps, and, looking up, saw coming towards him a tall, well-built man dressed very elegantly and carefully, carrying a camp-stool, an easel, a canvas, and a large case of paints. Just a little behind him came a lady in a rather soiled white silk blouse, with no hat, but with a band of black ribbon fixed around her hair. When they came within a few yards of Mr Wendover the lady said, "This is the place, Leo. This will do."

And the gentleman began putting up the easel, while she set her canvas on it and opened her paint-box.

Mr Wendover felt a little awkward, because he was so near to them that he would not be able to avoid overhearing everything they said, but, on the other hand, he felt that if he got up and went away at once it would look as though he did not want them there. So he sat still where he was. The lady began painting, and the gentleman sat down on the ground, and for a long time neither spoke.

At last the lady said, "It is annoying; there is a tree right in the middle of the picture, and I can't see behind it from here."

The gentleman was very much amused. He laughed and said, "My dear Lizzie, you can't want to put what is behind the tree into the picture if you can't see it. Or perhaps you would like me to go and look behind it and run back and tell you."

"Oh, but I am not putting the tree in," said the lady, taking no notice of his amusement.

"Not putting the tree in?" he said, laughing more than ever, and looking at Mr Wendover as though he expected him to laugh. "I carry the paraphernalia all this way and then you leave out some of the scenery! I must say I feel cheated."

"But the tree is right in the middle, and too tall to get it all in, so that it simply cuts the canvas in half. I can't do that."

The gentleman was really very much amused. "Now I think that would be rather attractive. Don't you think so?" he asked Mr Wendover. "My wife wants to leave the tree out."

"Yes, I think I should *like* the canvas cut in half like that," said Mr Wendover shyly, without smiling.

The gentleman got up and looked over her shoulder at the picture. "In any case, you know, Lizzie, I can't understand you painting a thing like that. Now if I wanted to paint this forest I should put in all the trees at least,

and a king and some princes going hunting, and
heralds, and certainly a princess on a white horse,
and a unicorn behind one of the trees. Wouldn't
you?" he asked Mr Wendover.

"Oh no!" said Mr Wendover eagerly. "I
would have a woodland scene by Bach, with
Diana, and her attendants in gaiters and bare
knees, and feathers in their hats."

The lady looked up at him and smiled. "Yes,
I like Bach, but he is so hard to play properly."

"One should make the little notes play themselves," said Mr Wendover excitedly, "and only
play the big notes."

The gentleman sat down again, this time
nearer to Mr Wendover, and offered him a Turkish cigarette, and they talked in a friendly
manner for most of the afternoon.

When it was time to go he packed up his wife's
things, and turning to Mr Wendover, who would
have liked to see the painting but had let the
right moment for asking to do so pass, he inquired if he were coming back along the road.
And Mr Wendover, not wishing to lose sight of
his new acquaintances immediately, said that
he was, and walked along with them. You
would not have thought when you saw them
apart that Mr Wendover would reach up to the
elbow of the tall gentleman, but, as a matter of
fact, when they were walking together he reached

further up than his shoulder, but the breadth of the gentleman's shoulders was very impressive

During the walk they talked very pleasantly. By the way, the names of the lady and gentleman were Mr and Mrs Harding. Whenever a car passed, Mrs Harding, who was very nervous of them, climbed up the bank, and her husband and Mr Wendover had to wait at the side for her until she came down. This amused her husband too. Half-way along the road he said suddenly, "Look here, Lizzie, there is no need for me to carry the canvas as well as everything else. You take it. She'll make me carry the piano out for her next."

"Let me carry something," said Mr Wendover.

"No, Lizzie must carry the canvas. She's lazy. You can have the stool."

Mrs Harding took the canvas, looked in perplexity at a wild rose she had picked at the edge of the forest, and then dropped it on the road. Mr Wendover, not exactly from politeness, but because he did not like to think of the flower on the dusty road, picked it up and put it very carefully on the bank at the side, but after he had walked on a few yards he reflected that the grass on the bank was almost as dusty as the road itself, and he went back and picked it up again. When they reached the house they were staying in Mr Wendover had still a few hundred yards farther to go, but they begged him to come in and have tea with them, and he was very glad to accept the invitation. He put the camp-stool down, and followed Mrs Harding into a room which contained two pianos—a grand piano and an old cottage piano with discoloured keys.

"Please sit down there," said Mrs Harding, pointing to a chair.

And after putting the wild rose into a vase full of flowers, and on the way back letting his hand rest caressingly on the keys of the piano, he sat down and they had tea.

"I mustn't stay long," he said, "because the lady I stay with will be surprised that I am not back to tea."

" But won't you play for us before you go? That was why I asked you in," said Mrs Harding —"because you spoke about Bach."

"I ought not to stay this time," said Mr Wendover, "and I cannot play without my music, and perhaps you have nothing here that I know. I don't know very much. But I have some of my music here with me, and I will bring it next time I come."

Mr Harding smiled. "You play something, Lizzie," he said.

She looked rather perplexed. "I can't play now, Leo. My hands aren't very clean. I haven't washed the paint off. What will you

play when you get your music, Mr Wendover?"

"I think I could play some Grieg," he said
modestly.

"Oh," said Mrs Harding, "I have some Grieg
arranged for two pianos. We will learn that.
Where is it, Leo?"

"At home, dear," said Mr Harding. "Perhaps
you would like me to run home to fetch it?"
He smiled at Mr Wendover. "You know, I have
to carry her piano here because the other one
has one or two notes missing."

"Yes, but they are in tune," said Mrs Harding.
"I tried them yesterday. You wouldn't mind
one or two notes, Mr Wendover, would you?"

"No," he said. "Does he play with you at
home?"

"No," said Mr Harding, "my rôle is only
patron of the arts. I'll see about the music,
Lizzie. If you can suggest where it will be, I
will write and ask someone to go in and get it."

"On the piano-stool," she said. "And, Leo,
since we are going to do all this, we might as
well get the tuner for the little piano."

"Yes," said her husband, laughing again.

After tea Mr Wendover went home, and Mr
Harding not only saw him to the gate, but
walked with him right to his cottage, because he
was going past it to the pillar-box.

78

The next morning Mr Wendover happened to be standing outside the cottage when, looking up, he saw Mr and Mrs Harding on the other side of the hedge. She smiled and said, "Oh, there he is!" and then explained to him that they had forgotten to ask him to come in on the following evening. Then they went along the road, Mr Harding carrying a knapsack on his back and she a sketch-book.

Mr Wendover was very much pleased at the invitation, and thought about it all the afternoon. And when he was having tea he began to wonder if it were possible to ask them to tea with him, and he considered the dimensions of the room anxiously. After tea, when he was sitting by the window reading his music, which he always brought with him on holidays to read instead of a novel, he saw outside the old woman with whom he stayed, and went out to consult her on the matter. He was in the middle of doing so when his attention was caught by the eggs in her basket, which she had been collecting.

"How very extraordinarily brown that egg is!" he said.

"Yes; one of the hens always lays brown eggs."

"Which hen?" he asked.

"That one over there; her name's Sarah," said the old woman.

Mr Wendover looked at the hen with interest.

"Would you be kind enough to save some of the brown ones for me by to-morrow? I have some friends I should like to take them to. I have never seen such brown ones. Have all the hens got names?" he asked, after a minute's reflection.

"Only three of them," said the old woman, beginning to walk away—"Annie, Lizzie, and Sarah; but it's Sarah that lays the brown eggs."

He forgot to make the arrangements for asking Mr and Mrs Harding to have tea with him, and did not remember it again until the next evening when he was on the way to their house. But he had three brown eggs, and he carried them along the road very carefully, two in one hand and one in the other. People who passed him, especially people who passed in charabancs, laughed at him, though there was really nothing to laugh at.

When he reached the house Mr Harding opened the door to him and said, "That's right. Come in. The music has come. We have had the front door at home battered down to get it."

Mr Wendover, who was unable to shake hands with him because of the eggs, smiled politely at the joke and followed him into the room.

"We have got the duets," said Mrs Harding;

"there are some others in the book too. We can do those afterwards."

Mr Wendover smiled and put the eggs into her lap. "Look what an extraordinarily dark brown they are!" he said. "One hen lays them like that."

Mrs Harding smiled. "Are they a present for us?" she asked.

"Yes," said Mr Wendover.

"Well, why did you bring three instead of two?" she asked with curiosity.

"I don't know," said Mr Wendover in surprise. "She laid three."

Mr Harding knelt on the hearthrug before the fire and began to make coffee in a little saucepan, and if the tiniest grain of coffee or drop of water fell on either the carpet or himself he wiped it off with a large clean white handkerchief. Then he put a box of Turkish cigarettes on the table, and they sat and drank the coffee and smoked.

"Just imagine," he said, "Lizzie doesn't know the difference between one cigarette and another."

"Doesn't she?" said Mr Wendover, looking at her.

"Upon my word she doesn't. Now, you would expect anyone to tell the difference between a Turkish and a Virginia, wouldn't you?"

"Yes," said Mr Wendover.

"Will you want the piano-stool or a chair?" asked Mrs Harding anxiously.

"Oh, a chair," said Mr Wendover. "I always have a chair."

"What a good thing," she said, "because, of course, we don't bring a piano-stool with us as well. Have you finished your coffee?"

"Yes," said Mr Wendover, putting his cup down hurriedly.

"We'll try the duet first, though I want to hear you play too."

"Oh, but I haven't brought my music," said Mr Wendover suddenly in dismay. "I was carrying the eggs and I forgot."

Mrs Harding looked thoughtfully at her husband. Then she turned to the piano. "Oh, well, it doesn't matter," she said; "we'll be sure to have something here that you will play." She picked up the books and gave him one of them. "The Grieg is the first one," she said, and sat down on the piano-stool.

Mr Wendover opened the book and put it on the shaky stand of the little piano. He looked across at her piano and fingered the keys of his own reluctantly, but then he drew up a chair and sat down.

"We can't see each other," said Mrs Harding, looking round. "Leo, you must give the signal."

Mr Harding stood up in the middle of the room. "I can't turn over for both of you, you know," he said.

Mr Wendover studied the page in front of him and then waited. You must picture him sitting there looking attentively at a spot on the wall and listening for the signal.

Really, considering that he had not played it before, they played it very well, only perhaps she was a little careless over the details and he perhaps too careful; but then he was exceedingly fond of Grieg.

And you know, the minute they had finished it she turned back to the beginning without a word and they began again. They went through the whole book before she turned from the piano, smiling at Mr Wendover and holding the cuff of her silk blouse, from which the button had fallen during the performance.

"Now you play something," she said.

Mr Wendover smiled at her too, and gave her a pin from the lapel of his coat. She pinned up the cuff, and he turned to look through the music. Then he exchanged the piano-stool for the chair, sat down gratefully at the grand piano, and played some Bach very nicely.

"Now mind, don't forget any of your music next time," said Mrs Harding.

After that they sat and talked for a short time.

When Mr Wendover went, they came out to
the step to say good-night to him.

"It is far too cold for you in a silk blouse,"
said Mr Harding, and put his arm round his
wife to protect her a little from the cold.

She pressed Mr Wendover's hand kindly.
"Will you be all right going along the road by
yourself?"

"Yes," said Mr Wendover.

"But don't the lamps on the cars dazzle your
eyes?"

"No, I don't think so," said Mr Wendover.

"All right. Good-night then, and mind you
bring your music next time. Have you got your
hat?"

"Yes," said Mr Wendover, showing it.
"Good-night."

As he went down the steps Mr Harding said to
his wife, "Come in quickly, dearest; it's too cold
for you."

Mr Wendover walked along the road. A taxi
rushed past him. Perhaps two people were
coming from a party, or perhaps two people were
simply arriving late at the hotel. When the taxi
had gone out of sight, it was so dark in the shade
of the trees that he could not see anything at
all. He had enjoyed himself immensely. When
he reached the cottage he found the key under
a stone, and let himself in without making a

sound. He lit the lamp, and the old woman's cat, sitting at the top of the stairs, watched him go up on tiptoe to bed.

That night it rained all night, and when he looked out of his bedroom window in the morning, though the rain had cleared a little, everything was very damp, and the trees looked very green, and there were no people about. After breakfast he put on his boots and his macintosh and went out for a walk. He walked along the delightful wet road towards the Hardings' house, but before he got there he turned into the path to the golf-links, between trees with noble, perfectly straight trunks and high branches dripping with rain. When he reached the golf-links there was nobody about, only someone in the distance looking for a ball in the wet grass. But suddenly it began to rain again; in fact it came down cats and dogs. Mr Wendover hurried to a wooden shelter just near, sat down on the narrow seat inside it and, putting his cap down beside him, watched the rain. And before very long he heard their voices, and Mr and Mrs Harding came hurrying into the shelter too. Mrs Harding took off her hat and shook it, and tried to tidy her hair with one hand, but left it in the middle.

"Do you like rain as much as all this?" asked Mr Harding.

"No, I don't think so," said Mr Wendover, standing up to welcome them.

"No, I can't say I do either, but Lizzie positively likes it."

"Leo, if you could fix this ribbon my hair would keep up," she said.

Mr Wendover watched her with great admiration. Her hair nearly all came down before she managed to push it up again, and her husband smoothed it with his hand and tied the black ribbon very skilfully round her head. Then they sat down on the seat and waited for the rain to stop.

A sheep came looking round the corner to shelter from the rain, and ran away in surprise at seeing them there, and soon afterwards a dog came running in, wet and out of breath, and he stayed, wagging his wet tail and shaking the rain off himself. And Mrs Harding's cuff, showing wet and rather soiled beyond the sleeve of her macintosh, still had the pin in it.

But the rain did not stop. Mr Harding pulled out his watch.

"We shall have to go through it or go without our lunch. What do you say?"

"I mustn't be late to lunch," said Mr Wendover.

Mrs Harding stood up and pulled her hat on, and they walked down the path and along between the tall trees, which were still thirstily drinking the sweet rain, the nectar from heaven.

It rained all the afternoon and all the evening, but the next morning it had cleared. Mr Wendover suddenly thought of asking the Hardings to tea, and, when he had consulted the old woman, he went himself to the shop to buy some biscuits, and a pot of marmalade which he happened to notice. Coming back from the village he went straight on to the Hardings' house to invite them.

Mr Harding opened the door and looked rather surprised to see him. Mr Wendover would not go in, but, standing on the step, began to explain what he had come for. Mr Harding looked at him a trifle absent-mindedly, and, turning heavily round, called, "Lizzie, here is Mr Wendover to see you. He won't come in." And in a most strange way he sat down on a chair near the door and looked past Mr Wendover along the road.

After a minute Mrs Harding came out of the room and came to the door. She shook hands with Mr Wendover and, keeping her hand there, looked at him while he explained what he wanted. She smiled a little absent-mindedly too and said, "Yes, we should like to come; shouldn't we, Leo? What time do you want us? What time shall we go?"

Mr Harding rather incomprehensibly took out his watch.

"Please come exactly at four," said Mr Wendover, beginning to walk down the steps.

Mrs Harding smiled and nodded. "Exactly at four."

And all the time they were talking, the biscuits they were to eat for tea were sticking up out of Mr Wendover's pocket and the marmalade pot was clutched firmly in his hand.

In the afternoon Mr Wendover sat by the window and waited for them. The old woman's cat came in and washed herself. They were a little late. He looked at the table and changed the position of the marmalade jar. But they came at last, and he watched them come through the gate and walk past the window to the porch. Mr Harding walked, looking straight in front of him, and she was looking up saying something to him.

They came in, and the old woman brought in the teapot. Mr Wendover begged them to sit down. The cat watched them from the window-sill. Mrs Harding noticed how skilfully Mr Wendover poured out tea. How pathetic it is when a man pours out tea so nicely!

"Please have some of my marmalade," he said.

"Do you know that we are going home on Friday?" she said, looking at him.

"The day after to-morrow," said Mr Wendover.

"Yes; we can't stay any longer. We have been here three weeks already, you know. How long are you staying?"

"Until Monday," he said, blinking a little. "Can't you stay a little longer?"

"No," she said; "Leo has to get back. In fact it is quite difficult for us to stay until then. Isn't it?"

"Yes," said Mr Harding, looking through the window.

Mr Wendover looked at her without saying anything.

"You had better come to see us to-morrow evening," she said, "since it is the last. Hadn't he, Leo?"

"Yes," said Mr Harding, looking round. "The piano need not be packed until the morning."

"Oh, thank you very much," said Mr Wendover.

"And I'll take all your music back with me to-night," she said, "or you'll forget it again. Remind me, Leo."

"It's all over there," said Mr Wendover, pointing to it.

Mr Harding behaved most strangely all the evening. That giant of a man with his nice clothes sat looking out of the window and hardly

spoke a word or made a joke, and once or twice
he passed his hand over his eyes as though he
had a headache. Once when Mr Wendover
reached up to the high mantelpiece and touched
him on the arm and said, "I bought Turkish
cigarettes especially for you, because I remembered that you always smoke Turkish," he said,
"The fact is, Mr Wendover, you think they suit
my character. You think I am a Bluebeard,
who will chop my wife's head off." But he so
quickly relapsed into silence that Mr Wendover
was even a little disconcerted. After that he
hardly spoke at all. Mr Wendover and Mrs
Harding did all the talking.

When it began to get dark and Mr Wendover
would have lighted the lamp, she said, "Don't
light it. It is light outside. Let us go for a
walk instead. I like this time of the evening.
Will you come, Leo?"

Mr Harding got up heavily and they went out.
They walked not among the trees but along the
road. It was the very beginning of twilight;
nothing had faded into shadows, but the sun had
simply gone. It was a kind of negative moonlight. And it happened to be quiet, so that it
was like taking a walk in the middle of the night.

Nothing eventful happened during the walk.
Mr Wendover walked along by Mrs Harding's
side, looking at her from time to time, and they

went right as far as the inn called the Three Dogs, and saw through the window two men drinking silently like two thirsty robbers from the forest. It was nearly dark when they reached the cottage, and the Hardings did not come in, but after thanking him they went home.

The next morning after breakfast Mr Wendover went for a walk. As he walked in and out of the trees he reflected that though it was a great pity they were going away so soon, into that evening would be concentrated all the enjoyment which he derived from their company, so that instead of having his impressions of them stretched over a long period, they would be in one complete picture, and that would make it easier for him to enjoy thinking about afterwards. He prepared himself for this climax by walking as far as the place where he first met them, as though to revise the first stages in their acquaintance. He was late getting back to lunch. When he got there he found on top of his music, which he had put on the table early in the morning, so that he should not forget to take it, a letter addressed to him. It was:

"DEAR MR WENDOVER,—I am so sorry, Leo had some business that he had to attend to, and we have had to go home to-day instead of to-morrow. It is a great pity, but it was imperative that Leo should go. That means that you cannot come to-night to see us. We are both very sorry to miss you. We have enjoyed your playing, and I hope we may meet again at some time.—Yours very sincerely, ELIZABETH ELLCOT."

Mr Wendover's heart sank. He sat down and ate his lunch, feeling acutely disappointed. He suddenly remembered that when he passed their house there was a gigantic packing-case outside; that was probably the piano. He had not realised then that it had a fatal significance. He propped the letter up against his glass and read it again. Suddenly he thought, "Why, what an extraordinary thing! She has put the wrong name!"

In contemplating this and in trying to find a reason for it a certain feeling of pleasure came back to him. "It is her name before she was married," he decided. "She forgot." After lunch he sat down and wrote her a letter.

"DEAR MRS HARDING,—I was of course much distressed to learn that you had gone, because I was looking forward to coming to see you this evening. I always come here for my holidays, but it is the first time I have met anyone interesting. From now to Monday it will be lonely. I hope your husband is quite well, and that the holiday has done him good. I always come here for my holidays, so perhaps if you choose this place again we may meet again, and I will always bring down any music I should wish to show you in case of that. Please give my best wishes to your husband. I hope he is well.—Yours sincerely, JOHN WENDOVER."

He took it to post, and walked along the road carrying it in his hand. But when he reached the pillar-box he remembered that he had to get the address from the house where they had stayed. On the way back to the house he began to feel depressed, and before he reached there he tore up the letter and did not send it after all.

CULTIVATED PEOPLE

In our town we have a Music Club. It meets every Wednesday night during the winter, and the ladies and gentlemen on the committee exchange musical confidences in public which they would in any case have exchanged in their calls upon each other, while the ladies and gentlemen who are not on the committee keep their programmes and compare them with one another until they are able to recognise a piece at the first few bars, and even name it unless it is called Op. and a number.

The president is a gentleman called Mr Challis. He has a bald head and exceedingly short legs, and he is not thin, and he has a passion for Tchaikowsky, especially for that song called "A Heavy Tear."

Last year the club was particularly interesting, because at the very beginning of October Mr Challis introduced to it as a member a German lady called Miss Wolf, who, moreover, played the violin. She had a rather fat, pale face, and small, very sad brown eyes, as though she had been a great deal alone.

Now I want to state emphatically that we would on no account have run an Italian, but there is something very appropriate to a music club in a German lady.

Mr Challis first met her in a concert. She happened to be sitting next to him, and on the two occasions when she dropped her programme he picked it up for her, though there was not much room and it was difficult to do so noiselessly. She thanked him in such excellent English, that he would never have suspected that she was a foreigner had she not been raised to such a pitch of excitement by the middle of the concert that she turned to him and said of the violinist they had come to hear, "If he only played *notes* he would be vonderful!"

After this, in the interval Mr Challis very discreetly inquired if she had been long in the town, and she not only told him that she had just come, but remarked also that she intended to give lessons in German, and in pianoforte and violin playing here. Just as the violinist reappeared on the platform Mr Challis asked her to join the Music Club, and after hesitating only a moment, begged her to accept him as a pupil for German lessons. She bowed silently, and they listened to the music again.

I do not know whether on that occasion she told him that she had already lived in England for ten years, but Mr Challis, though he, at any rate, knew of this later, treated her very much like a helpless stranger in a foreign land. There was an element of deceit, too, in his taking

German lessons, because he already knew German rather well; but of course one can always learn something more.

After the concert he was very much tempted to invite her to take tea with him in a café near, but he thought it was perhaps better not to do so, and parted with her after arranging to take his first German lesson on the following Wednesday at six o'clock, and he added, "If you should care to come to our Music Club, which is held on that evening, I shall have much pleasure in introducing you."

When, on the Wednesday, he reached the house where she lodged, he heard her practising on her violin, and he stood on the step listening with bowed head until she happened to see him through the window, and she came to the door with violin and bow in her hand.

"I am most sorry," she said; "I was playing, and I did not hear you knock."

"And I was listening, so I did not knock," said Mr Challis with a bow.

She led him into the room, put her violin down, and sat at the table.

"Have you learnt German for long?" she asked.

"Yes," said Mr Challis, smiling benevolently; "but there is so much I am unsure of."

"But where shall we begin?" she asked doubtfully.

"Perhaps we could read something, and I could ask you any question that would naturally arise out of the reading," said Mr Challis.

She looked at him more doubtfully and then stood up and said, "Very well. My books are all upstairs. I will bring some."

While she was away Mr Challis looked round the room, at the music on the piano, at the photograph on the mantelpiece of a gentleman who must have been her father, and at her slippers under the chair.

She came back with a large pile of books. "Choose," she said, putting them on the plush tablecloth.

"I should like to read some Heine again," said Mr Challis, and she sat down and they began.

At seven o'clock he looked at her questioningly. It was clear that she had forgotten all about the club. He reminded her of it delicately, and again begged her to let him escort her there. She looked at him in rather a tired way, but probably recollecting the necessity for meeting people and getting pupils, she agreed to come, and went upstairs to dress. As she drew on her gloves, Mr Challis added that she would be doing a great kindness if she would bring her violin and perhaps play to them once, and she consented to this too. They walked along the road, Mr Challis carrying her violin case.

And this was the first occasion on which she came to the club. Since it was the first meeting of the session, Mr Challis, as president, was in a very important position, and delivered a presidential address, in which he referred to the presence of a possible new member, and smiled at Miss Wolf sitting in the front row. And in addition to this he sang some Tchaikowsky in a bass voice, so that it was clear to Miss Wolf that she was acquainted with the most influential member of the club.

Towards the end of the evening, coming forward and bowing, he said to her, "We should be very pleased if you would do us the honour of playing for us, Fräulein."

She got up, took up her violin, tuned it up, and, as she was beginning to play, she turned to Mr Challis and said with a smile, "I am not inspired to-night."

Then she played some Glazounov. She played it beautifully. Mr Challis was in raptures, and went so far as to kiss her hand. And though everyone admired the easy nonchalance with which he did it, nobody dared to follow his example. But Mr and Mrs Gallon, his old friends, who with him had founded the club many years ago, came up and shook hands with her, and asked her to play once again; but this she would not do, and begged to be excused.

On the way out numbers of people thanked her for playing, and expressed sincere wishes that they should hear her again, as though they were all on the committee.

From that evening Miss Wolf found herself possessed of a most overwhelming popularity, and if she had accepted all the invitations to tea which she received, and remembered all the people who unostentatiously sat by her conversationally when she happened to come a few minutes too early to the club, she would have had neither time nor energy left for her lessons. However, she accepted the invitations only of the committee and recognised hardly anyone else. And people who wanted very much to know her but did not like to push themselves took lessons with her, so that she could not fail to recognise them. And she played nearly every week in the club.

The people she visited most often were, of course, Mr and Mrs Gallon. Mr Gallon was a small man, with a head which was flat at the back like a Dutch doll's, and he had black straight hair, which added to this resemblance. And to crown it all, he always wore hats which were far too small for him, so that you would have thought he was bound to notice it when he looked in a mirror. But perhaps he never did look in a mirror with his hat on, and yet surely he did when he bought it!

He possessed boundless musical enthusiasm, and played duets with his wife. Mrs Gallon was an excellent pianist, and played equally well on all occasions. Sometimes when she was alone or sitting unnoticed in the club her face would set into the most extreme ugliness, the ugliness of a peasant woman, and the misery expressed on it at those moments would never, even if it had been noticed, have caused any comment, because it is already something of a metaphor to describe it as misery.

The first time Miss Wolf went to call on them was one Sunday when they had invited her to lunch, and Mr Challis called for her and took her there. They went upstairs together, and while Mr Challis walked into the front room, the maid showed Miss Wolf into a bedroom, and for some reason left her there. She sat down on the bed and, looking at a framed text on the wall, began all at once to feel depressed and homesick, though there had not been any framed texts on her wall at home.

It was quite a long time before the maid returned and showed her into the drawing-room. It was a large room like a nursery, coloured buff and blue, and there was a worn carpet on the floor, and instead of a rocking-horse a large grand piano. Mrs Gallon, who was sitting by the window, and Mr Challis, who was in a basket chair in the corner, got up to meet her, and after that they sat down and talked. It was a beautiful day. Mrs Gallon and Miss Wolf looked out through the window, and Mr Challis watched them both from his basket chair.

"When my husband comes home we can have lunch," said Mrs Gallon.

"Has he gone to church?" asked Miss Wolf.

"No, he is just out for a walk."

"I think I can see him coming," said Miss Wolf, looking down the road.

Soon he came in and shook hands with Miss Wolf. Mr Challis for some reason hurried to her side as if to present her to him.

"Did you bring your violin?" asked Mr Gallon.

"No," said Miss Wolf.

"Challis, why didn't you remind her? What a nice morning it is."

He sat down on a stool and held out his hand to the cat, who climbed lazily on to his knee.

"Do you like cats very much?" Miss Wolf asked Mrs Gallon.

"Yes," she answered, looking out of the window, "I like them much better than human beings. But the cat I had for years died last summer, and I have not let any cat take his place since."

She got up and took a book out of the music-stool, and took two photographs out of it.

"Here he is," she said, showing them to Miss Wolf.

"Oh, he is most beautiful!" said Miss Wolf. "What was his name?"

"Thomas," said Mrs Gallon, looking at the photographs before she put them back in the book.

"And what is that one's name?" asked Miss Wolf, pointing to the cat on Mr Gallon's knee.

"Brahms," said Mr Gallon, looking up at her.

"Ach, Brahms," said Miss Wolf, laughing. She got up and stroked the cat.

"Borodin was very fond of cats," said Mrs Gallon on the way down to lunch.

"Yes, so I have read," said Miss Wolf. "What a very nice garden you have," she said afterwards.

"Yes, but it faces north," said Mrs Gallon.

"And we grow nothing but vegetables in it, you know," said Mr Gallon. "My wife won't grow flowers."

"But I assure you they are wonderful vegetables," said Mr Challis, helping himself to spinach.

"Winter will soon be here," said Mrs Gallon, sighing.

"You do not like winter?" said Miss Wolf.

"I prefer the summer. I spend all the summer out of doors. There is a wood not far from here. I go and sit there."

"And she stays there all day. She even forgets to come in for lunch. I suppose she lives on mushrooms and nuts," said Mr Gallon.

"I am very fond of mushrooms," said Mr Challis, "but, do you know, I have never, so far as I recollect, picked any."

When they had finished lunch Brahms followed them upstairs.

"Will you sing, Mr Challis?" said Mrs Gallon.

"Oh, but I cannot until someone has played an overture to inspire me," he said, with an air of being a little shocked at the suggestion.

"Please play something, Fräulein," said Mr Gallon.

"I do not often play the piano before people," said Miss Wolf. "I, too, need to be inspired."

"Then Mary and I must play a duet," said Mr Gallon, and put another chair at the piano. "I play the bass because it is easier."

"But psychologically more difficult," said Mr Challis, smiling.

They played some Beethoven. As they reached the end, Mr Gallon opened his mouth and curled his tongue, to express the extreme difficulty with which he finished on the same note as his wife. Afterwards Mr Challis sang, and Miss Wolf played some Chopin.

Whenever she was not talking or playing she looked out of the window at all the people going for a Sunday walk, and again, for some reason, she felt depressed and homesick, though there was in all this nothing particularly to remind her of home. Occasionally she leaned down to stroke Brahms, who was purring loudly on the floor.

After tea she and Mr Challis went home. The sun was beginning to set, and it was all golden behind the trees. Miss Wolf looking at it said, "I feel a little homesick to-day."

"Indeed I am sorry, Fräulein," said Mr Challis. "I hope you are not thinking of going back again and leaving us."

"Ach, no," said Miss Wolf. "Where should I go to? If I were homesick for Berlin then I should go there. But then before I lived there I lived in the country, but I do not want to live in the country. And since then I have lived many years in London. I do not know where I could go to." She sighed.

Mr Challis looked at her with sympathy as they walked along. "It is a beautiful evening," he said tentatively. "Would you care to take a little walk?"

"Please excuse me," said Miss Wolf. "I have at home some work which I must do. It is marking."

So Mr Challis merely accompanied her to her gate and then went home.

Of course Mr Challis saw her every Wednesday at his lesson, and almost always he took her afterwards to the club, except one evening when she had a terrible headache, and he was fearfully embarrassed at the thought that he had allowed her to give him his lesson. Also she sometimes went to concerts with him and the Gallons. At the beginning of December he asked her to tea in his own house, being very careful to ask the Gallons too, because he always paid great attention to the proprieties.

He had permitted himself to cherish the hope that she would arrive before them, especially as they were always late to everything except a concert. But because she had had some difficulty in finding the house she was even later than they, so that he spent the first few minutes of their visit in looking first at the door and then out of the window. The curious thing is that Mr Gallon did the same thing, probably from sensitiveness, and only Mrs Gallon sat and looked straight into the fire. Mr Challis was, unfortunately, a little deaf now, and when at last Miss Wolf walked past the window he did

not turn round and see her. Mr Gallon saw her,
but he did not say, "Here she is," which would
have been a quite natural thing to say, but
instead he looked hurriedly at the fireplace.

Mr Challis had a very nice house; he may have
expected it to make an impression on Miss Wolf.
She looked at his pictures very appreciatively.
And it was impossible not to connect everything
in the house with Mr Challis himself. When they
were having tea it was difficult to believe that
the cakes they were eating were not made by
him.

"May I go and ask your cook for the recipe
of these cakes afterwards?" said Mrs Gallon.

"Oh, certainly," said Mr Challis. "You know
she is new. The last one left to get married,"
he explained, smiling.

"The one I knew?" asked Mrs Gallon. "I
must send her a wedding present."

After tea she went to the kitchen. "I know
the way," she said to Mr Challis at the door, and
he came and sat down.

Miss Wolf took a cigarette from Mr Gallon's
case, and Mr Challis, bending down to light a
spill, lit it for her. They sat and smoked, and
did not talk much. Mr Gallon put his chin on
his hand and looked alternately at Miss Wolf and
at the fire. Mr Challis hardly looked away from
her, smiling all the time hospitably and with

delight at having her there. And she was very glad to be silent, because she had been teaching all the afternoon and could feel a headache coming on.

Mrs Gallon stayed a long time with the cook. She got on very well with cooks, and knew scores of them throughout the country. On holidays she would always penetrate to the kitchens of the hotels they stayed at. There must have been something in the personality of cooks which especially attracted her, because she herself never cooked when she went home, and rarely handed any of the recipes she had collected to her own cook.

When she came back they began at once to talk of the reception they were holding at the club after the new year. Miss Wolf was already practising her piece for it.

"Sing that song you once sang at our house," said Mrs Gallon suddenly.

"What song?" asked Mr Challis.

"I don't know what it was," said Mrs Gallon. "It went like this," and she began to hum on a high, piercing note, beating time with both hands and looking up at the ceiling. Mr Challis put his head slightly on one side and appeared to listen, but he did not remember it. The truth is that he had never been very much interested in Mrs Gallon. It was her husband he was really friendly with. In fact, numbers of people who know the Gallons like him best.

Mr Gallon listened very attentively to the humming and tried to recall the song, but he could not.

When they went, Mr Challis took them to the gate, and smiled and bowed as they drove off. Miss Wolf sat back in the dark car next to Mrs Gallon, until Mr Gallon helped her out and opened her gate for her.

"I thought you looked very sad to-night, Fräulein," he said, with his hand on the gate.

"Oh, perhaps I am a little homesick," she said, and turned to walk up the steps.

The Gallons and Mr Challis were away over Christmas. Before they went, Mrs Gallon and Miss Wolf met a few times to practise for the club reception; Mrs Gallon was playing the piano part. Of course on those occasions they did not talk, they simply practised. I do not think Mr Gallon met her at all; he happened to be out when she came there. But just a few days before the reception his wife sent him to Miss Wolf for some music, so he saw her then. When he went there she was out, but he went in and waited for her. He sat down in her room with his chin on his hand and looked at her slippers under the chair. She came in, and even put some parcels down on the table before she saw him.

"Oh, Mr Gallon!" she said.

"I am most sorry if I startled you, Fräulein," he said. "My wife sent me to ask if you could let her have the music for a day or two. She wants to have another look at it to make sure."

"Indeed she makes me feel ashamed," said Miss Wolf, going to the piano to get it. "She plays it already so well, and yet she practises it still more than I do. She is very good."

"Yes, she is good," said Mr Gallon, thinking of her. "But," he added, looking at Miss Wolf, "you are very busy too, I suppose, Fräulein?"

"Oh, not busy, but it is tiring to teach." She sat down. "Please pardon me if I put my slippers on."

"Certainly," said Mr Gallon.

Dear me, what nice feet she had!

"How is Brahms?" she asked, smiling.

"Very well, thank you," he said. "I hope you like musical receptions, Fräulein?"

"I do not know what this one will be like," she said.

"Oh, just like any other night, only there will be a place to smoke, and coffee, and it will last longer."

"The club in its Sunday clothes, *façon de*

parler," said Miss Wolf, looking at her parcels on the table. "Are you to play, Mr Gallon?"

"Oh no. But I am going to deliver a short address on Brahms."

"Not on your cat?" said Miss Wolf.

"No," he said, and reluctantly got up from his chair. "I will bring the music back," he added, standing looking down at the tablecloth.

"Oh, please do not. I know it now by heart."

"Good-bye, Fräulein," he said, standing on the step and looking at her feet on the mat.

"Good-bye," said Miss Wolf.

She came to the reception in a brown dress with a pattern of flowers on it. As she entered the room Mr Challis came to meet her, and kissed her hand again out of respect for Bach and Beethoven and Brahms, and because he felt excited.

"Where may I put my violin?" she asked.

Mr Challis took it from her and put it carefully on a chair. "If you will permit me to finish counting these cups I will show you," he said, taking his handkerchief from a pocket somewhere near his coat-tails.

Mrs Gallon came and she looked round once at the tables, but she did not help. If it had depended on her nobody would have had anything to eat or drink. But Mr Gallon went round putting chairs for everyone and talking to them. From the other end of the room you could see him opening his mouth wide and curling his tongue after he had told something funny. But Mrs Gallon sat down by herself, and on the face of that woman who never did any work, who played the piano all day, there was all the ugliness of the peasant woman who cannot live at all until she is ground between the stones and the earth.

Mr Challis took Miss Wolf out into the smoke-room and in through the other door to the platform to show her where she could put her violin. On other days there was no platform, but one had been fixed up and the piano lifted on it. Soon afterwards Mr Gallon gave his lecture on Brahms, and the concert began. Mr Challis sang. He stood on the platform and smiled as though he had invented the song and music itself, and even sound as well. And nothing could equal the anxiety he felt that everyone should like these things. Mrs Gallon played for him. Mr Gallon and Miss Wolf sat together in the front row and applauded afterwards. Miss Wolf played last just before the interval. She put the little pad on her shoulder and began to play. Mr Challis sat with Mr Gallon and listened to her. Ah, how beautifully she played! It was like a voice. It was wonderful that the violin could go up so high! Mrs Gallon sat down at the end of a table. She was thinking of the music they had been playing, and sometimes she beat time with a sandwich in her hand, thinking of some particular phrase of it.

Mr Challis poured out tea from the urn. "You cannot expect of a bachelor that he should pour out tea nicely," he said, smiling graciously down the table. "*Nicht wahr*, Fräulein?"

"Oh, you do it very well," answered Miss Wolf. She was thinking, "Why am I here? But wherever I were I should feel like this. The world is the same everywhere. One part of it does not belong to me more than another. I go where there are pupils. If I do go home the stones and trees are not likely to know me. It is all the same that I stay here. Oh, my God!"

"If you would like a cigarette, Fräulein," said Mr Challis, coming up to her afterwards, "please permit me to escort you to the smoke-room."

A number of plants and ferns had been placed there, and though it was merely a room, it looked warm and dim like a conservatory. She lit her cigarette, and sat in silence looking at the steps that led up to the platform, and Mr Challis sat sideways near her trying to begin the conversation.

Mrs Gallon was to play immediately after the interval.

"Is your music up there?" asked her husband,

coming up to her. "I had better turn over for you."

"I don't know," she said.

"Well, come and I'll open the piano for you," he said, and they walked into the smoke-room.

Just as they reached the place where Mr Challis and Miss Wolf were, Mr Gallon stopped suddenly and stared at them. Mr Challis was standing up, bending slightly to speak to her. It was clear that he was saying something very important. In fact he was saying, "If you could for one moment, Fräulein, consider me in such a way, I should be most happy."

"Oh, for Heaven's sake!" said Miss Wolf impatiently.

Mr Gallon did not speak, but walked straight up to them and sat down with them. He did not speak at all, simply sat down there in front of them to prevent them from talking together.

Mrs Gallon did not stop; she glanced at them and went on up to the platform. She picked up the music and opened the top of the piano, sat down and stared at the wall. People stopped talking and she began to play.

That woman thumping the piano up there, how is it that she can make such sounds? She has never played as well as this before at the club. She must have practised this piece very hard, perhaps for months.

Mr Challis came out of the smoke-room and sat down quietly on a chair near the door, and Miss Wolf next to him, and Mr Gallon stood at the door looking at his wife playing up there.

Everybody noticed how well Mrs Gallon played that night. As they went home people remarked to each other, "Didn't Mrs Gallon play well to-night?"

Mr Gallon packed the music and all the things into the car, and they took Miss Wolf and Mr Challis home as usual.

"Good-night," she said, walking up the steps.

Mr Challis climbed into the car and sat next to Mrs Gallon, and they drove off.

After this Mr Challis went away for a short holiday, and when he came back he did not go on having German lessons with Miss Wolf. And she does not go to see the Gallons as often as before. Of course, if she is playing at the club, and Mrs Gallon has to play the piano part, she is always wanting to practise, but Miss Wolf usually calls then in the mornings when Mr Gallon is out. She comes to the club nearly every Wednesday, and brings her violin from habit, so that she is nearly always asked to play, but people are beginning to say that she plays too often there.

SUMMER-TIME

The most foolish things happen to people in the summer. For instance, this summer a most foolish thing happened to Mr Joseph Laurel, and yet, of course, in a way it was a revelation too.

After playing tennis with Beatrice Hammond most of June and July, he went down to stay with her sister in the country. He dislikes tennis very much, but at the courts where they play there are on a sloping bank some lovely rhododendrons, and some large yellow flowers rather like them, growing on bushes, and with petals thick like wax and a heavy scent like honeysuckle. After about one set Mr Laurel flings his racquet on the grass and himself on the bank, and, with his hands under his head, he looks up at the sky or at the people on the courts. And there is something particularly luxurious about this, which the other players appear not to understand.

Beatrice is an extraordinarily good player. I suppose she plays to keep young, because she is well over thirty. Tennis is, if one might say so, very becoming to her. She is tall and dark, and it always seems like a sudden revelation of her personality to see her in white. And she moves like a winged fury behind the nets, and shoots stinging balls at people in a way that

Mr Laurel can quite understand other people finding rather fascinating.

She told him that her sister had invited him, but I should think the invitation really came from her. She said that they wanted someone to make up a set with her niece and her niece's cousin, and that she did not dare invite anyone who played well, because Leonora played so badly. And Mr Laurel, who prides himself on his bad tennis, decided to go.

He had been there before when the sister's husband was alive. They had a rather charming house, with a nice tennis court. The daughter, Leonora, had rather curious pale brown hair, the colour of smoke in a modern painting. When he saw her first she wore it down her back in ringlets. Now this time she had put it up in a rather old-fashioned way, which made her look older than she was. She had only just left school. The cousin who was there was also very young, a tall dark boy, very alert, and only just out of the sixth form.

Beatrice drove Mr Laurel down, and he was a little bored at first, but they had tea outside in the garden. Leonora sat opposite him in a green basket chair, near a rose tree, whose pink roses made her hair look strange. The cousin sat on the grass, handing the cake-stand round by balancing the whole thing from underneath on his hand, and though Mrs Chalen asked Mr Laurel one or two tiresome questions, all the same the charm of the garden began to make an impression on him.

"I want to ask your advice about Leonora," said Mrs Chalen, turning anxiously to him. "I don't know what to let her do."

"Has she any particular talents?" he asked.

"None that I know anything about," said her mother, looking at Leonora severely.

Mr Laurel looked at Leonora too, and she smiled back to him. She had a curious small, square smile, which was very attractive, though perhaps also a little heartless.

"She can't dance," said Basil, her cousin, not intending to insult her, but simply to eliminate one possibility.

"Or play tennis," said Beatrice a little impatiently.

"Will you have some more chocolate cake?" said Leonora.

"Thank you," said Mr Laurel, taking some. "I think she should go to an art school," he said to her mother.

"Do you really think so?" said she. "Can you paint, dear?"

"I don't know," said Leonora.

"Oh, that doesn't matter," said Mr Laurel, smiling at her. "Some artist will marry her because he wants to paint her hair, and they will live happily ever afterwards."

"Yes," said Leonora, with innocent approval.

"You really think so?" said her mother, smiling a little doubtfully.

"Undoubtedly," said Mr Laurel.

And thus her fate was decided, for sure enough she has gone to an art school.

"I am going to be a dancer," said Basil.

Mr Laurel does not remember much what happened that evening, but it was very delightful to see the darkness come slowly down over the garden and the roses.

However, that night, just as he was dropping off to sleep, he heard a little tap at his door, and then it slowly opened and Leonora's head appeared.

"Can I come in?" she whispered.

"Yes," he whispered back.

She came in, and Basil came after her.

"We are a deputation to you," she said.

"We are pleased to hear you," said Mr Laurel, leaning back on his pillow. "Switch on the light."

She sat on the edge of his bed. She wore a pink dressing-gown with lace on it, over her pyjamas, and looked very charming.

"Look here, Your Majesty," she said, "when Aunt Beatrice is here we have to play tennis all the time, and we don't want to."

"In truth," said Basil, balancing himself on the bedpost, "we, your liege subjects, flatly refuse to waste our time, and yours too, in such an unintellectual pastime."

He put his hands on the bed-rail and threw his legs high into the air, coming down lightly on the carpet.

"Now you have a good deal of influence with Aunt Beatrice," said Leonora, applying herself more seriously to the deputation.

"Sweet lady," said Mr Laurel, smoothing down the collar of his sleeping-jacket, "it shall be as you wish. We consider that the game is too frivolous for a royal pursuit, and will play it only when the Lady Beatrice, over whom we have no authority, absolutely insists."

"Good," said Basil. "Come, Leonore. Try to exit backwards. Good-night, Your Majesty."

But Leonora did not for the moment move from the bed.

"Is that your dressing-gown?" she asked. "Isn't it lovely? May I try it on?"

"A present from the Emperor of China," Mr Laurel remarked. "You may."

She walked up and down the room in the brightly coloured thing.

"It is curious how few colours suit you," said he.

She looked at him reproachfully and put the

dressing-gown on the bed. Basil switched the light off and went out.

"But when colours do suit you, they do," said Mr Laurel, laughing, and taking hold of the end of her dressing-gown. It slipped a little off her shoulder and she nearly left it behind with him, like the princess in the fairy tale, and she went out.

"Isn't he decent?" he heard her whisper to Basil outside the door.

Just as he was falling asleep it occurred to him that it was not a fairy tale at all, but Potiphar's wife. What an amusing thing!

The next morning he went into the garden before breakfast. They had breakfast very late there. The grass was still wet with dew, and the top of the tennis net was wet too. He drew his hand along it as he passed. Then he sat down in the sunshine.

Leonora and Basil came running down on to the lawn. She wore a navy blue jersey and knickers, while Basil looked very tall and rather diabolical in a black jersey and tights.

"We do our exercises now," he shouted in explanation.

They proceeded to do the more gymnastic dance steps. Basil seemed to be able to spring perpendicularly into the air with very little expenditure of energy. Leonora was agile, but there was nothing conscious about her movements. Basil turned a somersault on to his feet and said, "She helps me a lot, you know. I have to practise lifting her."

And he lifted her in various ways and into various positions, and finally, carrying her high above his head, he ran the whole length of the court with her.

"Bravo," said Mr Laurel, with genuine admiration.

"Do you really think it is good?" said Basil, coming back; "and it would be much easier with a proper dancer, you know."

"Yes," said Mr Laurel. "Have you any definite plans?"

"Well, not exactly," said Basil. "I have lessons every vac., you know, and now I can have them all the time. I shall have some money when I am of age, and Aunt Margaret is lending me some until then."

"Perhaps I can help you in some way," said Mr Laurel. "I know one or two dancers. Would it be any use your meeting them?"

"Oh yes, please," he said, and grasped Mr Laurel's hand. "Of course there is a lot I can't do, you know," he added. "There are many things I can't practise with Leonore. Look, put your hand there."

He placed Mr Laurel's hand on his spine and bent back very far indeed.

"Good," said he.

"Now do it to Leonore," said Basil.

He obediently put his hand on Leonora's spine and she bent back rather stiffly. If one could judge by touching it, her spine must have been very pretty. It is a funny thing, but there really is something very attractive about the thought of the skeletons of red-haired people. These are the only kind of skeletons one would not mind meeting at night. How deliciously intimate it would have been to have a conversation with Leonora's skeleton!

"You see, she does not press on you at all, as she should," said Basil, and Mr Laurel recalled the object of the experiment.

There was only one fault that could be found with the tennis court there, and that is that there was a glasshouse full of yellow roses just a little too near. When Mr Laurel does return a ball he usually endeavours to return it to heaven, whence at the beginning all things came, and on one of these occasions, after a short sojourn in the upper air, it fell through the roof of this glasshouse.

Leonora ran from her side to fetch it, and he, entering at the other end, contemplated for a moment the lovely picture she made among the yellow roses.

"How nice you look!" he said, forgetting to look for the ball.

She smiled. "Like what?" she asked.

I do not know why it is impossible to expound an æsthetic appreciation to a schoolgirl.

"Like the apricot and the pineapple in a fruit salad," he said.

She turned away, and as they both saw the ball and reached for it he pressed her hand, and the child blushed most furiously and ran out.

The curious thing is that he does not remember noticing Beatrice much during all this time. At least, they walked along together the day they went for a picnic, but she talked about the things they always talk about when they meet in town, and she rather got on his nerves, so completely had he given himself up to the atmosphere of the country and the garden and the roses, and Leonora with them. They were going to picnic on a little hill near, where some young birch trees grew near the top, rather like a regiment of young amazons, novices who, after the first battle, had been forced to retreat up the hill, but had retired in perfect order. A much older, larger tree among them added to this effect; but no, indeed, it made them look also rather like a party of schoolgirls with a mistress on guard, and they presented a most terrifying phalanx of virginity. Mr Laurel laughed.

They all sat in the shadow of the first of the birch trees and had tea, and afterwards he lay looking up at the sky and at the feathery little branches above his head, and listened to the sound of Leonora's voice making Basil arrange the things as she wanted them in the basket. Afterwards she came and sat by him, and began to fan him with a fern.

"The gnats are coming," she said.

Basil looked towards them, but seeing her occupied, called Beatrice.

"I say, Aunt Beatrice, if you could only hold this branch a moment," and he went out of Mr Laurel's field of vision into the big tree. But Beatrice on her way there cast at Mr Laurel a little smile of malice and veiled amusement, for which he saw no occasion then.

Leonora looked down at him and smiled, saying something or other, and he shut his eyes, and imagined himself making love to one of those birch-maidens, and slipping an arm around her slender silver waist. But as soon as he tried to imagine her virtuous reaction to such behaviour she turned back into a tree, with her little leaves and her branches swaying inaccessible above his head. He opened his eyes and looked at Leonora. She was looking at

him and she blushed a little. He wondered
what she would have done if he had slipped an
arm around *her* waist instead; but not for worlds
would he have had anything happen to dispel
the delightful languor of that afternoon under
the pale blue sky, so he contented himself with
holding a corner of her green dress as he might
have plucked a leaf of the birch tree.

They went home, not straight down the hill,
but along the side of it, by a path winding
between the trees. And he was no less charmed
with Leonora and the birch trees than with
Basil, walking between the trees balancing the
basket on his head, as dark and graceful as a
young slave.

By the time they reached the road it was growing dusk. Basil and Beatrice walked on in front,
and Leonora and Mr Laurel slowly followed
them. Leonora talked.

"I am so glad you have stopped teasing me,"
she said, and she told him all about school, and
her dearest friend Judith, with whom she had
only lately had a terrible quarrel, and about the
mistress whom they both adored, Judith, it
appeared, with a fierce and flaming passion,
Leonora, so he was led to believe, with a calmer
but more eternal devotion. And he learnt also
how serious a step she felt leaving school was,
and then he thought what a large gulf there was

between them, but not so wide that he could not help her to balance across it, perhaps on a thin plank that shook and dipped down in the middle. Not, you know, that he was nearly forty and she seventeen, but merely that he had left school a term before her.

It was nearly dark when they arrived home, and on the way into the garden Basil began to sing, beating time with a dusty branch in his hand, and Leonora joined in. Mr Laurel did not know the song, but he joined in too, singing anything to the tune. And again he caught Beatrice looking at him with a malicious little smile, which he resented without quite knowing why. It was a well-known fact that he did not always sing in tune, but he was not sensitive about that.

After this it poured with rain for three days without stopping. There was no tennis. Mr Laurel sat about indoors and read, and he spent one morning playing dances for Basil. One evening Leonora sang Elizabethan songs in a rather sharp, high voice. She stood in the middle of the carpet and sang without an atom of self-consciousness.

" You are more fresh and fair than I,
    Yet stubs do live when flowers do die,"

said her voice, and the piano played a little

126

dance measure to it. Really, it was all very charming.

The next morning the rain was over and the sun was shining through its tears. Mr Laurel went out into the garden. The grass was sodden with rain; three days' rain had fallen on it. The little posts on the tennis court were wet, and each rose in the garden was full of rain. There is something quite strange about a garden after the rain. A field wakes up fresh and strong like a peasant. Three days' rain is nothing to it. But a garden lies exhausted, like a young girl who has tasted too much the pleasures of love. There is no describing the voluptuous feeling a garden gives one.

Mr Laurel went and sat in a little summer-house and looked up at the house over the sloping lawns. And there he began carving a rose on the wooden table with such engrossment that he did not see Basil and Leonora come down to the garden, and they did not see him, but stood near a little rose tree. Leonora smelt a flower, and Basil handed her a handkerchief to wipe the raindrops off her nose.

He looked down at the flowers and suddenly round at Leonora. Then he looked up towards the house, but it never occurred to him to look in Mr Laurel's direction.

"Leonore, come over here a minute," he said, pointing to the glasshouse.

She looked up at him, but obediently followed.

Against the side of the glasshouse some freshly cut squares of turf were piled up. He pointed to them, and she sat down, looking up at him, and probably expecting some new trick. Now he was out of sight of the house. He bent down, put his arms round her shoulders, and kissed her, on the cheek though, not on her mouth.

Mr Laurel could see from where he was how she blushed. Basil laughed, and felt, I dare say, awfully wicked and daring. But he was a little embarrassed too. For lack of anything to say he kissed her again, and she hid her face against his macintosh. They sat down side by side, and could not even look at each other. Then Basil said something with a casual air, nonchalantly turned a cartwheel somersault on the wet grass, and they walked out through the gate, looking straight ahead of them, and with the mark of the brown turfs across the backs of their macintoshes.

And as they passed out of the gate it seemed to Mr Laurel that his youth vanished with them. He watched them walk along the road until they disappeared, and he was left behind with the rain-sodden garden. He felt an overwhelming melancholy within his soul, and yet it seemed, too, as if he were on the threshold of a thought that would console him, when, looking up, he saw Beatrice sitting reading just outside the house. She was in white again, ready to play when the grass was dry. He suddenly began to see why she had smiled with such malice. It was at the spectacle of him fatuously running after a schoolgirl, anxiously watching each little blush, as though blushes were not simply a physical characteristic of schoolgirls. He nearly blushed himself at the thought. It would have been far more appropriate if he had carried on a flirtation with Beatrice, who was nearer his own age. He suddenly felt even more alarmed. He recalled the number of times he had played tennis with Beatrice and taken her out, without ever having considered that she was of a marriage-able age. But now that he had discovered that he was himself middle-aged, he began to see that he had behaved in a most compromising manner. He almost ran across the lawn, intending in a few moments' conversation to efface his un-conscious behaviour of years. But he stumbled up the steps, and when he got to her he felt a little embarrassed, perhaps not unnaturally.

Beatrice looked slowly up from her book as though she believed he had come especially to tell her something. This put what he had meant to say out of his head, and after a moment's embarrassing silence he hurriedly looked down the garden and said, " It will soon be dry enough for tennis."

"Yes," said Beatrice, and after a moment looked down again at her book. And as he went in he saw her smiling to herself, so that he felt awfully foolish.

She took absolutely no notice of him for the next few days, except on one morning, when Basil and Leonora were out together she made him play tennis with her. He felt unusually tired and weary. When Beatrice played with him she always played without exerting herself, so that he did at least touch the ball now and then, but this time she exerted herself to play. Balls seemed to be hurled at him from every direction, and everyone of them seemed to be expressing contempt. She served balls that sped low along the ground, and he felt that he had forfeited her respect for ever. If only he had had the strength to return one of them! But the racquet hung heavily in his hand and he felt profoundly depressed.

Only the day before they were to go he thought of the long drive home with her, and he felt that it would be an ordeal too terrifying to be borne. He walked downstairs thinking of it with dread.

"A letter for your Imperial Highness," said Leonora, waving it to him and laughing.

Mr Laurel opened it, and, though there was nothing important in it at all, said with an expression of great consternation, "I must go home to-day."

"But we were going to give you a farewell feast to-night," said Leonora. "Oh, please, don't go."

"I am so sorry," he said, "but it is very important."

There was no mistaking her disappointment. And she and Basil paid him the utmost attention during lunch, but he was not to be deceived a second time. And then they took him to the station, and sat on the wooden fence and waved him affectionate and admiring good-byes.

Now he has decided to go abroad for the winter, because he finds that his diary is full of engagements with Beatrice, and he is only waiting to keep some quite inevitable ones and to take Basil to lunch with the dancers, and then he will escape.

SWEET GRAPES

My friend Hugo Ferris decided, a few summers ago, to taste to the full the pleasures of solitude, and actually answered an advertisement in the *Times*, and rented part of a house somewhere in the Peak district, and situated, he was assured, right on top of a hill.

On the way from the station the driver turned to him and pointed to a building, rather like a castle, but quite obviously built in Victoria's time, at the top of a steep hill. Ferris thought, of course, that it was of some local interest, but the driver explained that it was the house to which he was going. It is true that it did not look very big. It was rectangular, with square towers at each end, and it was the same height everywhere, with a castellated top and windows at regular intervals. But Ferris at once felt sorry that he had come, because there seemed to him something very vulgar and ostentatious about renting it as a cottage for the summer.

There was only a steep footpath up to it from that side of the hill, and the car had to go several miles round to approach it from the other side. Here the hill sloped very gradually right down almost to the horizon. The road led round the hill and then curved back, climbing, until it went straight across in the shadow of the ugly little castle. Here there were some cottages and a small shop where one might buy cigarettes. It was all very ostentatious, and he disliked it very intensely.

His reception at the house did not in any way reassure him. A thin, pale woman of about thirty-two, with straight, untidy hair and thin, drooping eyelids, came out to meet him. She looked at him from under her eyelids with her head slightly on one side, in a way which one might even call flirtatious, and which irritated him very much.

"My husband is away, and only my cousin lives here with me," she said, "so you will perhaps find it rather quiet, but please come in to talk to us whenever you feel lonely." And she walked lazily into one of the rooms.

Ferris was completely disillusioned over his scheme for solitary pleasure. I do not know quite what he had expected, and really I should imagine that the place was very suitable. For the owner had been dissatisfied with it as soon as it was built, and he deserted it at once, so that the whole place had been completely neglected, and in my opinion there is nothing so conducive to meditation as a general air of untidiness and neglect. And I find it very difficult to understand his dissatisfaction with the place, unless indeed what he was really needing was a marble temple on a hill, you know.

For another thing, he might have found the other people in the house very troublesome. They might have played tennis or had garden-parties, whereas this Mrs Lester seems to have been a very indolent woman, and she and her cousin lived very quietly. However, from the very first Ferris resented it very much, even because he had to use the same staircase as the two women, and was therefore often compelled to talk to them on the stairs. He tried to adapt himself to it all. He read a great deal, and went out for walks, and when he was indoors persistently ignored Mrs Lester's invitations, and was even, one gathers, quite uncivil in his efforts to avoid them. But they appear not to have resented his behaviour in the least, but seeing that he was of a studious and retiring disposition, probably put all this down to his natural shyness and reserve, and must have felt at once rather sorry for him and rather impressed by him.

He does not remember when he first saw the cousin, but she made at first no impression whatever upon him, except that he noticed that on that occasion she wore some rather pretty earrings.

Of course I do see Ferris' point of view, and that it is a great embarrassment when a young girl has lived so much alone without friends and has dreamed about the future and about love and all that sort of thing, and has made, as it were, a whole world of her own; and then suddenly someone who is not only a dream but also a fact comes into this world, and immediately this fact seems to her to fit exactly into the framework she has made, or, if it does not fit, she forces it to do so, and stands weeping and breaking her heart because she can neither give up the dreams nor the reality. Ah, dear me, youth is a sad and a beautiful thing! But of course I see Ferris' point of view.

At first he did not see much of the cousin—I think her name was Elizabeth—though he sometimes caught her staring at him with curiosity. She was certainly rather pretty, particularly when she looked down. She then seemed to be much older than she really was, but when she spoke or looked up at anyone there was something naive and childlike about her which Ferris entirely failed to find beautiful or even interesting. She was, of course, only nineteen.

There was a haystack in the field which separated the wall of the garden from the road, and Ferris used often to sit and read at its foot. The first time he spoke to her was when, one day, she came upon him there. She stopped suddenly when she saw him and said, bending forward eagerly to speak to him, "What are you reading?

Will you lend it to me afterwards? I am so fond of reading, and I have read all the books here."

"It would probably not interest you," he said, standing up.

It was a book on the eighteenth-century *Enlightenment*, and hardly likely to interest a girl of nineteen.

"Please do not let me disturb you," she said, blushing slightly. "Please sit down again."

He smiled, but naturally did not sit down again until she had gone.

And another day he was sitting outside and she came across the path and, after a moment, said, "I must send for some books. I don't know much about contemporary authors. What would you advise me to read?"

"I do not know much about them either," said Ferris, laughing at some thought of his own. "I myself would not think of reading anyone but Aldous Huxley."

"Oh, what has he written?" she asked.

"I do not think you would like him," he said, suddenly recollecting that she would not understand the conversations.

She flushed a little and turned away. Of course he had no objection to lending her a book, but he knew that most women only talk about reading, and that is merely the preliminary to talking about love.

The next day a curious thing happened. He was walking across the lawn after breakfast on his way out for a walk, when he fancied that he saw Elizabeth looking at him from the second window in the west tower, so that she must have been on the staircase. Quite without meaning to do so, he waved his hand to her simply from politeness. However, she had already turned away from the window and did not see this. Afterwards he went out along the road which runs across the steep side of the hill, and, when he had gone a few hundred yards, to his surprise he saw her coming towards him.

He said, "Have you been for a walk already since breakfast?"

"I was simply strolling about wondering in what direction to take a walk," she said, looking at him and smiling, probably, you know, gratified by his interest.

In that case, he thought, there must be a short cut from that road to the house, and he decided to look for it on the way back.

He stayed out rather long, and thinking of the short cut, he left himself barely time to get home to lunch. He turned through the only gate through which Elizabeth could have come, and walked diagonally across a steep field. However, there was not another gate as he had expected, but a thick hedge with no other open-

137

ing than a small gap. He struggled through
this, and found himself in another smaller field,
and there were still a few fields between it and
the house. It had a gate, but this was at the
opposite end to the house, and it was otherwise
surrounded by an impassable thorn hedge. He
was compelled to go back into the first field and
to take a different route. And after a great deal
of scrambling through hedges he came to the wall
of the garden, exceedingly hot, and quite con-
vinced that he had not seen her at the window.

But as he climbed the wall he saw on the
garden-bed below him the distinct mark of a
high-heeled shoe. This had an extraordinary
effect on him, and two or three times during the
day he remembered it very vividly, simply, however, seeing it before him and not connecting it
particularly with her.

After this he did not see her for a few days,
then one morning he went up to his room for
a book and afterwards started out for a walk.
She was standing just outside the gate looking
down at the point of her walking-stick on the
ground. She smiled up at him and said, "Are
you going for a walk? So am I. I hope we
have not chosen the same direction."

He smiled, rather uncertain of what she meant,
but they walked down the hill together.

"Are you fond of walking?" she asked.

"Yes," he said.

"I suppose you wander about alone a good deal?" she said, looking at him with a certain naive pity in her eyes. It is astonishing how young girls have not the faintest conception of the pleasures of solitude.

"I prefer walking alone," he remarked.

She stood still. "Would you prefer to be alone now?" she said.

"No, not at all," he said, and afterwards he put his book in his pocket.

He had intended taking the road which led away to the east, right over the hill again, about a mile farther on than the house, and when they came to the sharp turning he turned without thinking into that road. Elizabeth hesitated a moment.

"You perhaps wanted to go straight on?" he asked.

"No, this will do," she said, hurrying forward determinedly.

They walked up past a cottage with roses growing at the side of it, and a dog, lying in the middle of the road, got up half on his side and looked at them inquisitively. It was rather warmer than it had been during the past few days, but the sun did not shine so brightly; there were clouds, and the sky was a much paler blue.

They went right over the hill, and began to

come down the steep path on the other side into
the village. Elizabeth looked down at the path
as they trod on the loose stones, and, leaning
on her stick, looked exceedingly beautiful. Her
movements, too, were rather graceful, and she
stood very well when she stopped for a moment
to look at the village just below them. She was
tall, in fact a little taller than Ferris.

When they reached the bottom they walked
between two houses on to the road, where the
church is on one side and an inn on the other.
They were thirsty, and they went in to drink
something. The room was empty, and they sat
at a table by the window and drank ginger-beer.
The bar-woman went away and only a tortoise-
shell cat stayed with them. The cat jumped to
the bench beside Ferris, rubbed against the
corner of the table, nearly upsetting his glass, and
finally settled, purring very loudly, on his knee.

Elizabeth leaned across the table and stroked
the cat. She had an extraordinarily beautiful
neck. With her hand still on the cat she looked
up at Ferris and laughed. Then they both felt
a momentary embarrassment, but an embarrassment that did not bring them nearer to each other.
On the contrary, he felt for some reason a little
irritated with her, and he looked out of the
window for a minute.

Looking a little anxiously at him, she played

with her glass. Ferris, looking round again, saw her hand curved around the glass and very white against the grey ginger-beer. He contemplated it for a moment.

"You never wear any rings," he said in surprise.

"Do I not?" she said, smiling.

"You ought to wear rings. I do not like rings on nervous hands, but there is not a trace of nervousness in your hands. They are what I should call sophisticated hands, and you keep them still. Have you any rings?"

She stretched her hand half-way across the table and looked at it.

"Do you like sophisticated or unsophisticated beauty best?" she asked.

"Sophisticated, undoubtedly," he said, still looking at her hands.

She hesitated a moment, looking at him intently, and then said with a laugh, "Am I a type of sophisticated or unsophisticated— beauty?"

Ferris looked up at her so quickly that she hurriedly changed her expression.

"Unsophisticated," he said.

She blushed a little. "But why do you like sophisticated beauty?" she persisted.

He was beginning to feel a little bored, and very tired of the sound of the word.

"Oh, I do not know. I prefer so-called decadence in art too. It is merely a matter of taste." And he believed that he had dismissed the subject.

"But surely," she said, with pathetic insistence, "surely decadence isn't really nice?"

He was unable to restrain a gesture of impatience. She saw it, and must have realised all in a moment that she appeared to him very stupid. She opened her mouth to speak and efface the impression, but because, I suppose, she felt rather like crying, she closed it, and leaning back in her chair tried to keep the tears out of her eyes. And when he looked at her again she only half smiled.

"You look extraordinarily beautiful when you look down," said Ferris unexpectedly.

"Yes?" she said warily.

"Yes?" he repeated, with her intonation, and stretched his hand across the table. But as he did so he caught sight of the clock on the church tower opposite. It was already a quarter past twelve. He cannot bear being unpunctual, so they hurried home, but she could not have been the good walker she had appeared. She lagged behind him as if she were tired.

A few evenings afterwards he was sitting outside in the garden just before dinner. There was nothing there which one could really call a garden, for though the outer wall of the little castle enclosed a fairly large amount of ground, it had been, as I said, completely neglected. The garden therefore consisted of nothing but lawns, so badly kept that they were little different from the fields around, except that on the east side there were a few small shrubs, which, however, since the wall there was fairly high, were not visible from the steep side of the hill. And there was also, under the wall which Ferris had climbed that day, a flower-bed in which grew at wide intervals some rather sombre-looking fuchsias and a few stunted Michaelmas daisies. Here against the wall was a shelter of no great beauty with a green zinc roof, but there was in it a comfortable wooden seat and a table. Ferris was sitting here correcting an article when Elizabeth came up to him.

"Good evening," she said, smiling down at him and letting her hand rest on the table.

"Hullo!" he said.

She looked down at the seat beside him as if measuring something in her mind.

"Are you too busy to talk to me?" she asked. There was, unfortunately, something in her voice which reminded him of her cousin's.

"Yes, very," he said.

She wrinkled her forehead, but, smiling again, said, "Too busy to talk to *me*?"

"Yes," he said, but with a smile, so that she did not think it was the truth.

She sat down on the seat beside him. "It is a lovely evening," she said, looking at the gravel path.

Ferris looked at his wrist-watch. There was a moment's silence.

Then, turning to him suddenly, she said, smiling, but in a rather desperate whisper, "Would you like me to give you something quite unexpected?"

"Yes," he said, smiling too, expectantly and with curiosity.

She put her arm round his shoulder and kissed him on the mouth. He was quite astonished. He looked at her resting against his shoulder with her eyes closed, and then he bent forward and kissed a rather nice salt-cellar in her neck. It was surprising how beautiful she looked with her eyes closed. It had the same effect of making her look older. But it was a strange thing, because her eyes were in themselves beautiful enough, large and grey and very expressive.

She lay without moving. But from everything one must awaken. She opened her eyes slowly and with a certain languorousness that was very attractive.

"Well, my child," said he, "these proofs must be posted before eight o'clock."

She stood up quickly, resting her hand on the table. "Do you want me to go?" she said softly.

He pressed her hand gently and removed it. "Yes. Run along now," he said. "Good-bye." And he began to look for his pencil on the ground.

The next day after lunch he was sitting reading when she knocked at his door. She hesitated at the door, but came and sat beside him on the sofa, and put her hand gently on his arm.

"Have you been up on the tower here?" she asked.

"No," he said, putting his hand on hers to keep it there.

She smiled up at him rather shyly. "I could take you up there," she said. "Will you come?"

There seemed not to be much point in it, but he did not wish to refuse her. They went up the staircase, and then, through a door, up some wooden, perfectly clean steps, about which there was nothing very adventurous, and so out on to the tower. She led him to the wall.

"Isn't it lovely?" she said.

But, as a matter of fact, there was nothing to be seen from the top of the tower which could not be seen from the ground, because the house was so high up in any case. And since the tower

was exactly the same height as the rest of the
house, and there was besides, at the other end,
another tower exactly like it, there was no
sensation of being far above everyone. The
only thing was perhaps that by slowly turning
one could see all the views in turn, and this
gave one a better impression of the lines of the
hills curving into one another. Ferris began to
feel a little bored.

"Shall we go now?" he said.

She turned and came from the wall and
suddenly pressed quite close to him. He kissed
her. It was rather amusing to be kissing someone up there on the roof as if they were in a
nest. As he began to walk backwards down the
steps she put her hand on his shoulders and,
bending down, kissed him again.

As the holiday went on Ferris began to feel
more and more bored. He says that the scenery
was very monotonous. All the villages within
walking distance were very much alike, and one
had the suspicion that if one climbed the hills
opposite, to the south, one would see another
landscape exactly the same as the last, except
that there would be a slight difference in the
curving line of the hills. Whatever variety was
to be obtained they already enjoyed by having
a steep slope on one side and a gradual slope
on the other. But I myself think that solitude

does not really suit him. There are some people like that. They seem to be very retiring and even unsociable, and their whole intercourse with their fellows is merely a little intellectual conversation. But that little is a necessity; without it they can exist least of all men.

And of course I quite understand that his relationship with Elizabeth did not provide any suitable conversation. And yet one would think that a young girl growing up there, with her soul opening out, so to speak, hanging on the lowest bough waiting to be plucked and all that sort of thing, would be rather nice. But of course that is quite a different thing.

It seems that Ferris spent the rest of the holiday simply bored. He was tired of going for walks, he read a little, but more often he merely sat waiting for the holiday to be over. It is often so with holidays. One becomes so much refreshed that one can scarcely exist for the last few days without work.

The day before he went she said to him, "What will you do when you go home?"

"Do?" he said in surprise.

"Yes," she said. "You are going to-morrow, aren't you?"

"Yes," said Ferris, still a little puzzled. "I shall work, I suppose."

"You won't be able to kiss me then, you

know," she said, smiling, but with a very anxious look in her eyes.

For some reason Ferris thinks this was very funny. He laughed then, and he laughed very much again when he told me.

"Won't you be sorry?" she asked gently.

He became serious, and reflected for a moment. "No, on the whole, I shall not," he said truthfully.

The tears came to her eyes and she looked down at the grass. Of course it was fearfully embarrassing for him. I believe he walked away or did something like that.

The next morning he went away. He shook hands with her and was very kind, but she stood at the door and did not speak a single word. He says she did not look at all pretty that morning. I do not think it has occurred to him that she probably cried in the night. Of course it was all very awkward for him, and it is not easy to fit in exactly with a young girl's ideas of life, for it is for her still very much like a fairy tale, and yet it seems a pity that something so like a flower, like a young rose, you know, should have to cry all night.

A GARLAND OF EARTH

I AM an old man now, and I do not know whether I am able any longer to tell a story without making unnecessary observations. Perhaps, too, I am seeing subtleties that were not really there, and yet it must be the fault of the old that they see too little in life, not too much.

I was one day walking along the street in one of the northern towns when a man carrying a large brown-paper parcel, and though he was short, stooping very much, came towards me and, looking always at the pavement, walked right into me and nearly knocked me over. He mumbled an apology, and bent down to pick up his parcel, which had fallen. I leaned for a moment against the wall to regain my breath. As he stood up again he peered up at me with his eyes half closed. He wore no glasses, and he was not old, but he must have been very short-sighted. Suddenly he grasped my hand and said, "But, Mr Leonard, sir, don't you know me?"

I looked at him again, and it was quite true that I knew him. He was the son of an old schoolfellow of mine, and twenty years ago, after his father's death, when he was a student, he used to visit me. And he reminded me, too, how when he got his first work he used to come to dinner with me on Sundays. That was very true. He used to come every Sunday until he met the lady he afterwards married.

He was engaged at present on some very important work, so he told me. His wife was dead, but he had two children, a daughter of seventeen and a little son. And he was anxious for me to see them. He did not live in the town, but near a little village on the coast. It was very stormy there in winter, but better for his daughter's health. His little son, too, was home. He had been ill, and would not go back to school until half-term. He begged me to come there to pay them a visit.

"I have been very successful," he said, walking by my side, half on the pavement and half in the gutter. "And I owe much of it to your kindness." He peered up at me again with half-closed eyes.

I remember that I did help him once. I paid his fees for an extra year at college. But I have forgotten what it was, and he paid it all back. It is a pity that such a young man should stoop like that; I do not stoop so much although I am nearly twice his age.

I promised to visit him. In two days' time he would again be in the town, and he would take me home with him.

I was able to buy a fan for his daughter and

a book by Herman Melville for his little son
before I went there with him on a Tuesday. The
village near which he lived was very small; all
I observed of it was a semicircle of houses built
of almost black stone around the small bay, and
the pale, hard sand in the bay was the only sand
visible for miles along the coast, for everywhere
there were rocks, and on the farther side of the
village was a high cliff. From one side, too, a
small stone pier had been built jutting across the
bay, and at the end of it was a black tower,
perhaps the first part of a lighthouse left un-
finished. It was very much like a chess castle
but without a castellated top.

However, before we came to the village we
turned away from the sea, and after a short climb
we reached the house, a fairly large one, built
of the same black stone as the village houses,
but to one side of it had been added in lighter
stone a long, low building with many windows,
the whole of great ugliness.

Coleman looked up at me, and, pointing to the
low building, said, "That is the laboratory."

There was not a tree anywhere near, and one
could see the sea from the windows.

When we entered the house, Coleman stood
at the bottom of the stairs and shouted the
announcement of my arrival. The first to
answer was his son, a little boy in an Eton suit.

"This is Jimmy," said his father.

The little boy shook hands with me, and, looking up at me with bright brown eyes, asked, "What did you do at school, sir?"

Now I thought that he meant by what exploit or adventure was I remembered in my school, though it seems that he really wished to know if I had done algebra and Latin in those far-off days, so I answered, "I carved my name three inches deep on the organ, Jimmy."

"Golly!" said Jimmy, and his face expressed the most intense delight.

And I think, indeed, that from that moment he conceived a certain affection for me. I hope, however, that when he returned to school afterwards he did not repeat the act, because it was a good organ, and I have since regretted it.

Coleman's daughter came next, walking slowly down the stairs. She smiled, and shook hands with me over the banister. She was a very pale girl, with pale grey eyes and fair hair, in itself very beautiful, standing up from her head as a certain type of dark hair does. But although she was so young it was pinned up at the back into a knot.

Her father put his arm round her thin shoulders. "This is my scientist," he said; "she knows already more than I can teach her. She will be another Curie."

She smiled. "But, papa, you must let me show Mr Leonard his room."

"Yes, of course," said Coleman, taking his arm away.

Rahel—that was a very pretty name she had—Rahel and I began to walk upstairs. Jimmy followed, pulling my bag after him. My room was very pleasant, with two large windows looking towards the sea and on the left across the bay.

I opened my bag and gave Jimmy his book. I do not know whether Herman Melville is too old for a boy of eleven, but Jimmy immediately sat on the top of the stairs and began reading it. That was good. I had brought for Rahel a very beautiful fan, the kind of present that it is a great pleasure to buy. I gave it to her.

"You must realise that I cannot feel anything but affection for the daughter of your father," I said; but I must confess it was something of a pretty speech, though I had a great affection for her grandfather.

She took the fan and looked up at me seriously out of her pale grey eyes. Then suddenly smiling, she took my hand and said, "Thank you very, very much. Nobody has ever given me a present like this before."

But she put the little fan into her pocket. She did not hold it up to her face before the

153

mirror. When she had gone, I sat down in the armchair in my room looking at the sea. But while I looked I fell asleep without knowing, and only awakened when Jimmy came up to call me down to tea.

Rahel was there. She had just taken off an overall covered with stains, and it was lying on a chair near her.

"Papa will come in a minute," she said. "Mr Froud is staying here."

"Do you like the book?" I asked Jimmy.

"Yes," he said, "only there is rather a lot of —what do you call it when someone talks about things for three or four pages?"

"Description?" I said.

"No," he said; "it begins with f."

"F, f?" I said, reflecting.

"Here is Mr Froud," said Rahel in a whisper. A young man had come into the room. He had a small, wide face, with round eyes almost like a frightened owl, and he hesitated in front of us as if he really were frightened. Rahel presented him to me, but afterwards he almost ran to a chair, and did not speak a word until Coleman entered, and then he hurried into a serious conversation with him. It was clear that they were engaged upon some work together. For a few minutes I listened to them, but Jimmy said suddenly, "It's filosophy!"

"Ah, f," I said. "That is quite true. It is full of philosophy."

It seemed that Rahel had been ordered by the doctor to do no work with her father that summer. She was to keep out of doors and go for walks. So during all the time I stayed there we three went for walks together, and both these children were very kind and considerate of me, although I think that I walked a little slowly for them. But Rahel always carried a tin specimen-case with her and collected botanical specimens, and she said that she was making a map of the flora of the district. I remember when she first told me about this, and I said, "Ah, yes, of course, pressing flowers."

She looked at me in surprise, and with perhaps a little impatience. But I had meant only that she was the modern equivalent of the young ladies of another generation who pressed flowers. I am no opponent of the higher education for women.

Occasionally Mr Froud joined us on these walks. He walked on ahead, and came back to us sometimes to make some observation.

Once when he was with us we went through the village and up the steep cliff on the other side, where there was an old ruined castle built on the very edge of the cliff. It was very cold up there and windy, so that my scarf blew again

and again up into my face. But Mr Froud wore
no overcoat and appeared not to notice the wind.
We went right up to the ruined castle. One of
the walls rose sheer with the cliff itself, and from
its windows one looked down far below on to the
rocks and the sea. There was a story that from
one of these windows a nurse had let fall a baby,
the only son of the house. And from this window
we looked with horror on the cruel pointed rocks
so far below.

"I bet he bounced," said Jimmy, upon whom
the tragedy weighed light.

Another time we went along the stone pier to
the little chess castle, and Mr Froud came with
us then. We all stood inside it. It had simply
the open door and two little spaces for windows,
one looking out to sea and the other to land.
Mr Froud looked out through each window, then
he said, "If you were a prisoner in this and you
could have only one window, which would you
have?"

"The sea one," said Rahel, without hesitating.

"And you?" asked Mr Froud, turning to me
with great eagerness.

"The land window," I said, looking through
it at the little village and the rocks and the pale
sand. "One would at least see one's fellow-
creatures."

"But that would make it worse," said Rahel.

"I'd choose the sea window," said Jimmy in a muffled voice, "because you can escape through it." And it was with difficulty that he was prevented from achieving this.

"And you?" I asked Mr Froud.

"I don't know," he said quickly; "I am sitting on the fence."

It seemed to me a curious metaphor to use in such a matter, and it brought an amusing picture to my mind.

We went for walks, and I saw for the first time in my life many flowers that had always been too small for me to notice. They grew in the short coarse grass, and did not seem beautiful at all, but when Rahel picked them and showed them to me before putting them in the tin case, I could see that they were of great beauty—tiny, exquisite pink flowers that lay almost invisible at one's feet. It is true that a scientist does not see their beauty, but there is enough that is beautiful in the world to last all one's life's days.

That Mr Froud, too, was a curious young man, though it was not possible to hold a conversation with him. Sometimes he would come into the room in a short, dirty, very wide blue overall, and, looking at me with round eyes, he would hurriedly sit down on the piano-stool and play with his acid-stained fingers. And sometimes,

if he played Beethoven, for example, it seemed
to me that he played almost with inspiration.
But he never went all through any piece. He
would suddenly get up again and hurry out of
the room. But he might have made a musician.
I suppose he was very clever. He had a very
great admiration for Coleman, and in many ways
it was amusing to see him trying to restrain his
eager impatience when Coleman talked to me;
and more often he did not succeed in restrain-
ing it, but plunged headlong into some scientific
argument. He had also a great respect for
Rahel, would often be overruled by her opinion,
and once said to me with great emphasis and
even awe in his voice, "She is a genius, you
know."

But there was to me always something strange
and sad in this pale girl of seventeen looking at
Mr Froud with her pale grey eyes, and his round
dark eyes looking down at her with that mixture
of respect and impatience.

The truth is, I think, that the only one in the
house whose temperament was in any way akin
to mine was Jimmy. We used to have tea
always in the entrance-hall, a little room with
windows of small diamond-shaped panes of
brown and green glass. And Jimmy and I very
often had to wait here for the others to come
from the laboratory. And on one of those

occasions I asked him what was his favourite subject at school, and he answered that it was composition, and that he liked best to write it on his favourite book. Now that was excellent, because after all he is only eleven. But I remember very well that that was also my favourite subject when I was a little boy.

But I had also the greatest affection for Rahel, and she, the young girl, showed an affection for me, and talked to me and even sought my company as if I were her father.

I remember once I went out by myself, and since it was a dry, windy day, when I came to the village with its semicircle of little black houses I went down the steps on to the beach, where it was more sheltered. The sand was quite hard and dry, and almost white in colour. And there I came upon Rahel and Mr Froud. He was standing talking to her with his hand held out in a strange, absent-minded way, as if he had meant to take hers and had forgotten half-way. I hesitated a moment, but she saw me and smiled at me as I came nearer.

She said that she would come for a walk with me.

"Will you not also come?" I asked Mr Froud.

But he did not answer, and stood staring from one to the other of us with an expression of what one can only call stupidity. But it was not the stupidity of a stupid man, but that of an animal.

He *was* something like an animal, but some curious animal that I do not know. Perhaps, like the little flowers, it is something that has always been too small for me to see. Perhaps insects stare at one like that with round eyes. I have had a long life, but there is very much that I have not seen.

Mr Froud walked back towards the house and Rahel and I began to walk on. The poor little girl looked pale and strained. I put my hand on her shoulder and said, "You won't spoil your pretty head by too much studying, will you?" because I felt sad to see her.

She looked up at me and smiled, but did not answer. She likes me, but she cannot answer me because she thinks that I do not believe in the higher education for women. Ah, what barriers the young build around themselves!

We went across the sand to the other side of the little bay and then she walked over the rocks. The wind blew her fair hair as she turned to help me over them. It is not easy to walk over rocks, and I was never an athlete. When I was young I was a student. We sat on the short grass just above the rocks and looked out to sea.

A little to the right, where the rocks were

lighter in colour, grew a sea-pink. I looked at
Rahel anxiously, but she was looking at the
waves and had not seen it.

"Will you do me a little kindness?" I asked her.
She smiled a little and put her hand on my
arm. "Of course," she said.

"Well, please do not pick that little flower,"
said I.

She looked at it and smiled, and perhaps she
thought of the higher education again.

"Have you read William Morris' *Life and
Death of Jason*?" I asked.

"No," she answered.

"It is many years ago since I read it," I said,
thinking of those days. "There is a little sea-
pink in it, a little sea-pink growing on the
shores of Greece and looking up to sea."

"Yes?" she said.

"You do not know any Greek?" I asked.

"No," she answered, "only Latin, and not the
literature, only the language."

"Ah, that is a great pity," I said. "And, you
know, it is not the Greece of groves and night-
ingales that is so beautiful, but the Greece of
rocks and the sea, the Greece of the sailors."

"Yes?" she said.

I looked round at the little bay and the chess
castle at the other end, and the rocks and the
waves of the sea, and at the lovely little flower

on one side of me, and the girl with her pale fair hair and her pale face and her pale grey eyes. Ah, that was a moment of the greatest beauty!

After this I did not see anything so clearly.

One afternoon we all went for a walk up the hill at the side of the bay and along the cliffs past the ruin. All, that is, except Coleman. He worked always. We walked along a narrow path sometimes quite near the edge of the cliff, but sometimes, where the cliff jutted out, a few yards from it. And on the largest of the little promontories we sat watching the waves breaking on a sandbank a hundred yards out to sea, and the gulls circling and screaming over the rocks. Mr Froud, half lying on his side, dug with his fingers beneath the short yellow grass, and then stared intently at whatever he had found. But Rahel, except that she held a few poor little flowers in her lap, looked out to sea. And Jimmy, on the other side of me, with his chin on his hands, gazed too with unwonted quietness at the waves.

The sky was grey with large greyish white clouds, and there were moments when even the white foam flying into the air and the circling flight of the seagulls seemed to rest in their movement, petrified into the calm of everything around.

We stayed there for a long time. Then gradually from the other side of the bay there came a great black cloud. It rose up slowly, gathering strength as it came, and, like one of the Erinyes, stretched its grey hands above us and called to its sisters to follow, as if it brought to one of us the vengeance for some blood-guiltiness, but as if it, too, felt the horror of the doom it brought.

"Hadn't we better go?" said Rahel.

"No, no," said Mr Froud, sitting up quickly. "That is absolutely nothing. It will pass over the sea and not touch us."

"But Mr Leonard," said Rahel, looking at me anxiously.

"I have a coat," I said, not wishing to spoil their pleasure. "And perhaps it will blow over."

Mr Froud sat looking at the cloud. The wind began to rise, and he breathed it in with pleasure and excitement.

"I suppose it can't be very nice to be in a ship when a big cloud like that comes all over you," said Jimmy. "It makes *me* feel small, so I don't know what a *ship* must feel like."

"But a ship is bigger than you, Jimmy," said Rahel, smiling.

"Yes," said Jimmy, reflecting. "But it is lower down, isn't it?"

"Yes, that is very true," I said. "It is lower down."

There were no people in sight besides us, and

the Erinyes do not visit their vengeance on nature but on men. The great cloud came nearer and the wind rose higher.

"Now we *must* go," said Rahel, looking at Mr Froud.

We got up and began to walk quickly along the path, Mr Froud following us, and looking back longingly now and again to the place where we had been sitting. But we did not escape the rain. When we were half-way home it came pouring down. I begged Rahel to have my coat, but she would not; she only consented to shelter from the wind by walking just at my side. Jimmy, who might have run quickly home, walked thoughtfully in front of us. But Mr Froud, his black hair quite wet because he wore no hat, almost skipped along on the grass beside us, and every now and then shouted to us remarks which the wind carried away in the opposite direction.

"A mistake . . ." we heard above the wind, ". . . perspective . . . the sea."

When we reached home Rahel ran immediately to change. They were all quite wet. Only I had had a coat. I went up to my room, and suddenly feeling tired, sank, a little dazed and troubled, into the chair. Outside the sea was dark grey, and it still rained heavily.

Jimmy must have come quietly into the room,

for suddenly I found him in his pyjamas staring up at me.

"Hey," he said in surprise, "you haven't even taken off your hat!"

I took it off, and also my coat.

"Rahel said I was to fetch anything you wanted dried."

I sat down again. "I am not wet. My coat is long."

"Excuse me, please," said Jimmy, and stepping up to me felt the place beneath my necktie.

"Yes," he said, "that is where your coat does not close. I will wait."

And afterwards he carried my woollen vest down to be dried. And I wrapped my dressing-gown around me and went to sleep in the chair. I believe that Mr Froud was playing the piano downstairs.

I have had a long and a pleasant life. But how can I know what will come before it is over? These few years that I have yet to live will bring something as new and strange to me as anything these children have before them to see. One comes, an old blind man, like old Œdipus at Colonos, leaning on the arm of a girl, looking down with blind eyes on the earth, and suddenly one sees little pink flowers, like children looking up to the sky. One may not rest yet, one may not rest yet.

A THRONE IN HEAVEN

Sidney Mihail intended to be a poet. He used to sit at the dormitory window when the other boys were asleep, and look at the garden and write stanzas and stanzas in his diary on his knees. The moon shone down on the garden, on the laurels, and on the bed of irises by the wall. The irises were not deep purple as in the daytime, but black in the moonlight. And the moment he saw this he could write a poem about it—he hadn't to wait to think. He could begin writing it down at once. In the holidays he walked about by himself in the garden. There was a horse-chestnut tree there. In winter the buds stood on the ends of the branches like iron, but in the summer it was covered with leaves and the pink flowers. He sat under it and wrote in a big book he had. In the headmaster's garden, where he was allowed to walk in the holidays, were two rows of Madonna lilies. He walked along the gravel path in front of the lilies, and they all looked at him, like a procession of tall, wicked nuns pushing out their worldly golden tongues.

In the holidays there were no boys in the school, only perhaps one or two little boys whose parents were in India. It is easy to talk to little boys. He did not sleep in the dormitory in the holidays but in a room, and he went in his dressing-gown to the little boys' room and told them ghost stories until it began to get dark.

Afterwards all the boys came back to school again. Those very pink flowers on the chestnut tree were now chestnuts, and the boys pelted each other with them. They were brown and hard. Oh, holy snakes!

Snowdrops came out and crocuses, and then daffodils, and soon it was summer again. Out in the country in the little woods there were bluebells, and sometimes garlic began to grow there, and the white flowers drove the bluebells back, like a white cloud hiding the blue of the sky. He could hardly wait to get back to school to write it down. He wrote some of it under the table at dinner while they were waiting for the pudding. The red valerian grew again by the water-tank in the yard. His favourite poet at that time was Rossetti.

And then he got the first prize for literature, and his essay was printed in full in the school magazine. And before the holidays this time he was invited to go and stay in the north on the moors for the summer. He had no guardian, properly speaking, only the lawyers, but this man had known his father, and must have been reminded about his existence in some way.

The journey there was very wonderful. He

had not even been in a train for years—not since
he went back to school after his father died. It
was terrible to look away from the window even
to write it all down. He wrote three poems.
Even when it got dark and he was a little tired
he kept his face against the glass, and looked at
the gleam of the rails, and the sparks from the
engine, and at lights here and there in houses.

At the station Mr Merrill met him. Sidney
did not remember him, but he said that he had
seen him when he was a little boy. He was
sorry that he had not realised before that he
was in school and alone. But he had had many
worries.

"I have a little daughter about your age," he
said, rather sadly though. "You will be good
company for her if you don't mind playing with
a girl. Do you?"

"No, sir," said Sidney.

Mr Merrill was looking carefully at the dark
road, because he was driving the car himself, but
he talked too. He told Sidney that they lived
there in the country only because of his daughter's
health. It meant that he could come home only
at week-ends and sometimes on Wednesdays,
because his work kept him in the town; but it
was much better for her here. And it was very
good for her to be out always in the air; they
must go for walks together. He felt he could

even trust him not to let her do anything silly
—not to get her feet wet or catch cold in any
way, because of course she never thought of her
health—a child like that. And he seemed a quiet,
thoughtful boy. But if he became tired of the
society of women and began to feel like that
of men, he need only come with him to town,
and they would have a few nights out like old
bachelors.

"Yes, but I am really very fond of nature,"
said Sidney gravely.

Mr Merrill turned to look at him, but he was
sitting with the rug pulled up over him, looking
with sleepy but wide-open eyes at the road.

Then they came to the house, a dark house
at the side of the road. A woman opened the
door to them.

"I had to let her stay up," she said. "She
was so excited."

"All right, all right," said Mr Merrill; "they
can both stay late in the morning."

Elizabeth came out of the lighted room and
led them in. She was a pale girl with short
dark hair. She was very excited. She whispered to him all through supper.

"You are very fair and I am very dark," she
said. "That is very suitable, isn't it?" And
she said about the woman, "She was really our
servant when my mother was alive, but I call

her my old nurse, because it seems more appropriate. Don't you think so?"

"Yes," said Sidney, but he was very tired.

"Hush, my child," said her father, putting his hand on her head. But she could not keep quiet.

"I am so glad you are pale too," she whispered, as they went upstairs. "You make me look quite healthy. They make an awful fuss over me. It is all nonsense."

He was so tired, his eyes closed by themselves as he went up the stairs. He opened them again all the time and looked round at her. She followed her father to his room with him. There beside his bed was a glass jar with a bunch of wild flax in it.

"Hannah said you wouldn't like them, because they are not really flowers," she said, "but I put them there afterwards. I love them."

Sidney smiled at her, but he was too tired to say a word. He shook hands with her and with Mr Merrill, and the very minute he got into bed he fell asleep.

When he awoke next morning it was already late. He got up to look at his father's watch in the pocket of his coat; he had forgotten to hang it by the side of his bed last night. He dressed himself and thought a great deal. Before he was ready Elizabeth knocked at his door and called to him. Hannah gave them breakfast together downstairs. He was a little shy at first and did not know what to say; he was not much used to the society of women.

Afterwards he and Elizabeth went for a walk. She hurried eagerly along the road; it was wonderful to have someone to show the place to. They turned out of the road first of all through a very tiny pine forest, and then over a little wall of black stones. Three small paths lay side by side; the short yellow grass on them was trodden down and the black earth showed underneath. On either side were whinberry bushes. His name for them was whinberry—in the north they call them bilberries—and those nearest the wood had not a single leaf left on them, and instead they were covered with caterpillars, striped in yellow and black, on every single stalk as though they grew there. But farther up there were plenty of berries, dark blue with a grey veil over them, and you know that each little berry has a dent at the top like a tiny carved goblet.

There were pools, too, here and there, and it was easy to get your foot into them before you knew it, because the heather grew all around them, and then only suddenly you found the deep holes in the black peat, and the water in them was wonderful to drink. There was wild

flax too, as though it floated on the air just above
the surface of the moor. A long way ahead at
the other end of the paths was a black stone
wall, and right up by the wall were even some
ferns and a few harebells. That day the sky
was all a dull white. Oh, it was wonderful,
wonderful!

They walked up the paths and picked whinberries and ate them. They are such beautiful
little things. And they are beautiful, too, when
they are still green. She went jumping over
the little bushes to pick the wild flax, and he
went after her slowly.

"You mustn't get your feet wet," he said.

She laughed, and went jumping across the
bushes right up to the wall. Close to the wall
the little bushes grew like a miniature forest, but
here and there were ferns, and then a space of
pale thin grass, and one or two big grey stones
and the little harebells growing beside them.
Nothing there had so light a colour as the harebells.

They sat down on the stones. They needed
only to stretch out their hands to pick the
berries. Her lips and her hands were already
stained blue with them.

"Do you like school?" she asked.

"I don't know," he said. "Yes, I like it, but
it is a difficult place to live in."

She thought for a bit. "What are you going to be when you grow up?" she said.

"A poet," he answered, and looked down at the ground, not from shyness, but of course because he knew the importance of what he said.

"A poet!" she repeated. "Do you mean that really?"

He nodded.

She was silent again and ate some more berries, but she looked at him once or twice. She had very dark grey eyes, so dark that they were almost black.

"What are *you* going to be?" he asked suddenly.

"I don't know exactly," she said. "I expect I shall get married, but I mean to stay here always."

"Perhaps you won't be able to," he suggested.

"Yes, I shall," she answered. "Even if my husband has to work in London we shall live here, and he can come for week-ends. Father does it."

"Yes," he agreed; "but it takes a long time from London."

"Oh, well, it needn't be London," she said; and then added in a questioning voice, "Of course, our house here is rather old-fashioned. Didn't you think so?"

"No, I didn't think of that," he said.

"Well, perhaps that's all right," she said doubtfully. "But haven't you noticed Hannah calls me Elizabeth? She won't call me Miss Elizabeth, and she wasn't really my old nurse at all; she was the servant, and now she is the housekeeper. What do you think?"

"I don't know," he said; "but I like her. I think she is good-looking for a middle-aged woman, and I think she suits this place."

"Do you really?" she said, and thought for a bit. She arranged the flax she had picked into a bunch again, and they were silent for a long time. "But have you written any poems?" she asked suddenly.

"Yes, of course," he said; "otherwise, you see, I shouldn't know that I was going to be it."

She did not ask him any more questions, and soon afterwards they went home.

They had dinner together, and Hannah stayed in the dining-room to talk to them. She had taken a liking to Sidney.

"It's a pity you're not as quiet and well-behaved as he is," she said to Elizabeth. "She's more like a tomboy than a girl. I don't know what Master Sidney thinks of you."

Sidney looked up at Hannah earnestly and he said, "No, I think it suits her to be as she is."

Hannah shook her head. "She's vain enough

now without her hearing such things," she said.
But she had not really minded that he said it.

After dinner Elizabeth had always to go and
rest, and to-day Hannah made Sidney go too,
but only because of the long journey the day
before. Another day he could do as he liked.
He went and lay on the bed, but he did not
really sleep. He read Rossetti for a bit.

> " Alas ! the bitter banks in Willowwood,
>   With tear-spurge wan, with bloodwort
>   burning red :
>   Alas ! if ever such a pillow could
>   Steep deep the soul in sleep till she were
>   dead."

Oh, how wonderful, how beautiful it was!

Elizabeth stayed for half an hour on her bed,
but she could not sleep, and she went quietly
downstairs to the kitchen, where Hannah was
washing up.

Hannah was angry. "Go back to your room
this minute," she said.

"Only one thing," said Elizabeth, putting her
finger on her lips. "It won't take a minute.
Shall I ?"

Hannah turned away with the cups to hide
her curiosity.

"He said you are the best-looking middle-aged
woman he has ever seen," said Elizabeth.

"That's nothing to come down out of bed to

say," said Hannah. But she wasn't angry. Oh no. You could see that by how nice she was to Sidney afterwards.

In the evening they played draughts. He hardly ever won. He was slow, and thought about it, but she had had so much practice. She always plagued Hannah to play with her in the evenings, and when her father was home naturally he played with her. But it was she who got tired of it first.

"Do you like reading?" she asked.

"Reading?" he said.

She could not wait for him to answer. "Do you like poetry better than books?" she asked.

"I don't."

"But it is something quite different," he explained. "Poetry you read over and over again for itself, but you read a book through for the story and to hear about other people. I like it very much."

"I'll lend you a book then," she said suddenly, shutting up the draught-board in the middle of the game.

He picked up the draughts which had rolled to the floor and followed her to the bookcase.

"I like Jules Verne, really," she said, "but I think *Lavengro* will suit you better. Have you read it?"

"No," he said.

They sat at the table and read. But she was nearly at the end of her book, and when she had finished she wanted to play draughts again. But he wanted to go on reading, so he went up to his room and brought down for her Rossetti's *Hand and Soul*, a beautiful copy in brown leather with red letters on it.

"I will let you read this," he said. "This is a book which is like poetry—you read it for itself."

But why it was called *Hand and Soul* he did not know.

They had to go to bed rather early—just the same as in school.

In the morning they went up to the little pine-wood again, but this time with a basket to pick whinberries for Hannah. It was so beautiful, it was a pity to have to leave it at all.

"If you can find me a big pine-cone I can make you a thyrsus," he said.

"What is a thyrsus?" she asked, looking round about the trees and bending down to pick little cones from the ground.

"I don't know exactly," he said. "It is Greek, but it is in Swinburne. It is what the followers of Bacchus carry, and in pictures it looks like a pine-cone tied on the end of a stick."

"Yes, I should *love* to have one," she said. But she could not find a big enough cone, and they had to pick the berries and go home. But he promised to come there in the afternoon, when she was asleep, and make one for her.

Immediately after dinner he went there again and wandered around the trees, and at last he found a cone big enough, and he sat down on the ground where the roots of a large tree showed above the earth, and began to bind it with string to the top of a stick. He did it very carefully, but it was not easy, and it shook and rattled a bit when it was done. He put it on the ground beside him. Then he took a Shelley out of his coat pocket and began to read *Prometheus Unbound*. The little pine-forest was as quiet as if it were night. He did not move except to turn a page, and the little thyrsus lay quite still on the earth beside him. He suddenly thought of Elizabeth as she looked when she was trying to find pine-cones, only he saw her with a long grey dress bending forward as with some great burden; the trees were upright, but she bent forward, always looking on the ground. In this wood was a magic pine-cone, and it was a spell upon her to look for it for ever and never find it. He put the Shelley down on the ground with the thyrsus and began to write the poem. It came so easily flowing in upon him. Afterwards he read again, but when he came to

" Life of life ! thy lips enkindle,"

he read it over and over, until at last he put the
book back in his pocket and held the thyrsus
tightly in his hand and thought for a long time.
And then he went home.

In the week-ends Mr Merrill was there. They
went out for long walks with him. One Sunday
they went along the road for miles and miles.
The road was beautiful ; it went right from their
house, it was wide and white, it went curving
up across the moor and you could see it for
miles ahead. Here and there at the side of it
were houses built of black stone. But they went
farther than the houses, farther up until the road
went across the flat moorland into a little hollow,
and then up once more to a church at the top
of a steep hill. It was already one o'clock. The
church was empty. Everyone had gone home
to his Sunday dinner. They went inside. Mr
Merrill showed them the seats for the choir-boys,
which were of beautifully carved wood—this
church was famous for them ; but up above the
altar was the window, not a rose window or a
crucifixion, with deep purples and crimsons and
greens as in some churches, but a row of saints
all in bright clear colours. Sidney looked up at
them, at the pale yellows and reds of their
dresses and the black lines where the folds were.
That was so beautiful !

They went out again. Mr Merrill and Sidney

sat on the seat in the porch to rest a little, but Elizabeth ran along the paths and began jumping over the graves. Her father called her and she came running back.

"Only a wicked, cruel girl would behave like that in a churchyard," he said, looking down at her.

"Why?" she asked.

"Would you like to think that somebody was jumping like that over your mother's grave?" he said.

She hung her head, but then she looked up at him again with her grey eyes. "But I wouldn't mind if anyone jumped over my grave," she said.

And this time he turned away from her, not as if he were angry, but as if she had really hurt him with something. She moved sideways to look at him and smoothed his coat with her hand, but as they went out through the gate she whispered to Sidney, "I am even wickeder than he said, because there were some white violets growing on one of the graves and I was dying to pick them."

"Oh, whose grave was it?" he asked.

"On '*Here lies Jeremiah Hopkins,*'" she began, and went along the road in front of them singing the rest of it, "and '*his dearly belovèd wife Sarah Jane,*' and '*his dearly belovèd sons William Henry and Thomas James,*' and '*his dearly belovèd daughter Louisa Mary.*'"

Sidney laughed and ran after her. He put his fist into his other hand and laughed again, and said, "When I die I'll have white violets put on my grave and you can come and pick them."

"What are you children talking about?" asked her father, smiling.

They stopped suddenly in alarm. She looked at him reproachfully.

"Why, she is very fond of white violets," he said, looking up innocently at Mr Merrill. "She said so."

She turned her dark grey eyes to him, and began to laugh with her fingers pressed to her lips.

"I shall be a bent old woman walking with a stick and with my head nodding, but I'll jump over your grave all the same. And just think how old father will be!"

"But perhaps he won't be there then," said Sidney, looking at them both.

"He will," she said, and ran to her father, and for a second put her face against his coat sleeve. Then she walked home quietly by Sidney's side.

And afterwards in the evening they played cards and talked, and went to bed late because it was her father's day at home. But even then Sidney could not go to sleep. He took out the thick book into which he copied his poems and he began to read what he himself had written.

That is a wonderful thing to do, and he had only
to look up from the book to see, as if it were
really before him, the stained-glass window in
the church, but between the saints in red and
yellow was another saint, and it was Elizabeth,
in the long grey dress with a huge bunch of
white violets in her hands, and she was leaning
forward from the window and laughing wick-
edly out of her grey eyes. There was something wrong with his church. And he began
to write the poem, *The Legend of the Wicked St
Ethelreda.* And when he had written the last
verse he was so sleepy that the eyelids dropped
over his eyes, and he put out the light and put
the book under his pillow and went to sleep.

The days went by one by one. Once Elizabeth
found him writing in his big book, and she
snatched it up from the table and held it tightly
in her arms and ran as quickly as the wind up
the road, and he in horror went running after
her, until they came quite tired and breathless
to the little pine-wood, and she gave it back to
him without ever once looking inside.

"Is your poetry in there?" she asked.

He nodded.

They sat in silence for a long time. Then he
said, "If you would like it, I'll read you one of
them."

"Oh yes, please," she said, and put her chin

on her hands and looked seriously and gravely
into his face.

He read one of them—an old one he had
written in school. She listened, and afterwards
she looked at it where it was written down. He
felt that he ought to show her one that he had
written here, and he did not like to show her
The Legend of the Wicked St Ethelreda, but he
read to her the one about the magic pine-cone
in that very wood. And this was wonderful to
her. She looked from one side to the other, and
said over and over again, "And it was *really* here,
where we are sitting *now*?"

And every time he said yes she was more
full of wonder. And he had to read it for her
again, twice—no, three times.

And immediately he thought of a new song.
A follower of Bacchus should sing it to a pine
tree asking for its fruit to make a thyrsus, the
follower of Bacchus with purple grapes and a
leopard skin, and the great pine tree in the
snow and the brown cone.

He gave Elizabeth his Rossetti to read so that
he could write it down at once. She liked *Sister
Helen* best—best of all in the book. That was
just what you would have expected of her. She
loved black magic and all wickedness.

Only once he went to town, and that was in
connection with a secret. It was, as a matter

of fact, to buy presents—a pair of gloves for
Hannah, a pipe for Mr Merrill, and a book for
Elizabeth, but he meant to give her his own
copy of *Hand and Soul* as well.

But the days went. When it was almost time
to go away again Mr Merrill talked to him, and
told him that he must come there every holiday
if he liked. He was so sorry that he had not
known about him in these last years.

"Perhaps you find it lonely here," he said,
"and in the winter Elizabeth is sometimes very
ill, so that she could not play with you, but if
you like to spend your Christmas here you
must come."

"Is she too ill to read?" he asked.

"No," said Mr Merrill.

"Then we can read together," he said. "I
will come whenever you allow it. And I will
write to her from school."

And when it was really the day for him to go
Hannah was sorry, and Elizabeth was dreadfully
sorry. She stood behind the door and cried, and
she was pale. Her father waited out in the car
for him, but Sidney had to stand by the door and
tell her that he would come back at Christmas
and always in the holidays if she liked, and he
begged her to read *Hand and Soul*, and to go
now upstairs so that she could wave to them as
long as the car was in sight.

DAYS

Mr George Morn, the novelist, began to write about the people and the scenes of the district around his old home only when he was already over forty, and almost as soon as he had begun to be recognised for these novels as a very great artist, it suddenly seemed to him that all he should ever want for the rest of his life would be to live among these old scenes, and he immediately bought a house a few miles from the house where he was born, and since then he has hardly been seen or heard of.

The house that he bought was exceedingly ugly, built of dark stone. There was certainly no idea of beauty in the mind of the man who designed it. All around it was a high wall enclosing a garden full of stones. And outside the wall the road curved over the stretches of short grass with a certain monotony.

George Morn came here in January, and he strolled through the cold rooms and walked about the country in the biting wind, and so far from noticing any of this ugliness he was overjoyed at being there, and his new novel, which he had intended to work at as soon as he came, was not even begun. He visited again the old places where he had played as a boy, and felt within himself a new energy and power, which it would be difficult to describe to anyone.

It was not until his wife wrote to say that, after giving a concert in June, she would be able to stay there with him for the three summer months, that he began to see that, objectively speaking, the house was really ugly, and even gloomy and depressing. He went out into the garden with her letter open in his hand and looked around him rather desperately. It was evening, and the moon was shining in the cold sky. It seemed to him, however, that something could be done about the garden.

The next day he sent for a boy from a cottage nearby, and together they took nearly a week only to carry the stones away. This was Easter Week. Afterwards the boy went back to school and could help only in the evenings, and Morn did all the digging by himself. After a day's work outside he would go in, his boots covered with earth, to the Golden Cock, which was not far away, for a drink and a smoke, and then come home, read some Voltaire, and go to bed. After a few days of this, with the invigoration of a giant he began his novel. He worked in a room at the back of the house, by a window looking on to a lawn of coarse grass, in the middle of which was a dead rose tree. There was no shelter there and no bud ever came on the tree.

But Morn never noticed it. Through an ugly little gate he could see the country outside, just where the road curves into sight. He forgot about the garden, and it remained all the year like a badly ploughed little field of poor soil, and some more stones had been turned up. As the summer came the earth began to look dry, but some grass and a few harebells grew on it.

On the morning of the day that Leonora came there a letter marked *urgent* arrived for her, and she opened it as soon as she arrived, without taking her hat off. It was from her friend Alexander Sorel, asking if he might come there to see them. He had long wished to meet her husband, and had always been very enthusiastic about his books. She wrote immediately asking him to come, and Morn added a very cordial postscript to her letter, reflecting that their guest could talk to Leonora all day and would not be likely to interfere with him.

During the first days after she came he worked very hard. He read the first few chapters to her, and this made him write more quickly. And she collected the loose sheets of paper on which he wrote and put them in order, and re-copied what was necessary. He wrote neatly and legibly, but he inserted scraps of paper in so many places that her help was quite necessary.

It was not at all warm, and it rained, so that she did not go out. He could hear her practising sometimes in the drawing-room, but the rest of the time she sat with a book open on her lap, not reading, but looking at her hands or thinking. It seemed to her that she had not had time to think for years. She had the curious feeling of living over again some of the days of her girl-hood. There was the same quiet and solitude as then. She used in those days to have a music lesson once a week, and except for that she did nothing after her practising but sit, as now, and think. Only then she sat, as it were, at a window always looking out and always expecting some-thing, whereas now everything was settled for her and nothing new could come from the out-side. Then it was for the meaning of *her* life that she anxiously scanned the passers-by ; but now, as one gets old, it is not the meaning of one's life but of life itself that one tries to under-stand, looking at one's hands or on the same black-and-white page of a book. That was the difference. There seemed, too, to be something pressing heavily upon her, but it was almost pleasant not to have to throw that feeling quickly off.

The day that Alexander Sorrel came the rain stopped, and she went in the morning for a walk by herself. He came in the afternoon. She

saw the car coming along the road and went
to the gate to meet him. He came hurriedly
out of the car. He is a little man, and
there is something doll-like about his clothes.
His collars always look very high. He was
already very much excited. He greeted her,
but he looked anxiously around the garden. He
had the most extreme admiration for George
Morn. But the comical thing was that when
Morn came out he hardly looked at him, but
even while they were shaking hands he glanced
nervously about as though he expected some
of the men and women in the novels to come
out of some door, or from behind some tree, and
eventually he addressed his remarks into Morn's
coat. And Morn, who has very bright blue eyes,
looked down at him in a way rather amused,
but then he hurried back to his room.

That evening Alexander Sorel began earnestly
talking to him about the novels, but within a
very short time he stopped asking questions.
As one who has expected to find an authority
on something and finds only a more superficial
knowledge of the subject than his own, he listened
with respect and consideration to the remarks he
had called forth, and then allowed the subject
to change. After this he took all his questions
again to Leonora, though he showed the utmost
respect and affection for Morn, which had

nothing at all to do with his opinion of his views on æsthetics.

The day after he came he and Leonora only sat out on the lawn, he with a rug over his knees, because when the sun disappeared for a moment behind a cloud it was very cold. They did not read, and they spoke only sometimes. But the next day, with all the air of a pilgrimage, they started out to visit George's birthplace. They did not suggest that he should come with them. There would have been something rather funny about asking a man to make a pilgrimage to his own birthplace, almost as though one should invite him to visit his own grave. Leonora had not been there for many years— only once since she went there the first time.

They walked along the road. Morn could have seen them from his window until they came right to the end. After that they turned down to the right along a steep path into a valley. Here there was an old farmhouse, and by its side some tall trees much greener than anything up there. It is the setting, too, of one of Morn's earlier novels. Alexander Sorel was looking about him eagerly.

"Laura lived here, you know," said Leonora.

"Ah, did she?" said Sorel, and he hurried up the path of the garden and stood peering into the dark passage.

Leonora stayed at the gate and stroked a cat sleeping on the wall. The sun shone slantingly across the garden, so that the front of the house was left dark, but the cat had chosen the sunniest place on the wall. Someone lifted up a curtain at the window, and then a woman came out to see what was wanted. She was a thin woman in an old black dress and an apron, with a pale, hard, austere face, and pale, almost colourless eyes.

"I came only to see the house," said Alexander Sorel.

An old man came walking as quickly as he could into the garden, so curious to know what was the matter that he walked past Leonora without seeing her at all.

"What does he want?" he asked.

"Wants to see the house, father," said the woman.

Alexander Sorel turned round to see the old man and shook hands with him.

"Thinking of buying it, perhaps?" said the man.

"No, it wasn't that," Sorel explained. "I merely wanted to see the house. You know that George Morn, the writer, lives near here, don't you?"

"Yes, he's the writer," said the old man, even with some pride. "Knew him when he was born."

"Well, I am staying with him," said Sorel, "and I wanted to see this house because the heroine of one of his novels once lived here."

"My family has always lived here as far back as anyone remembers," said the old man doubtfully.

"But it's only pretending, father," said the woman. "Not a real woman, but in the book, out of his head."

The old man looked round at her rather contemptuously, but turning again to Sorel asked, "Which room did she live in?"

"That, unfortunately, I don't know," said Sorel; "but perhaps this lady knows." He turned round to look at Leonora. "But don't you know her?" he asked in surprise.

"Can't say I do," said the old man.

"She is the lady who has come to live with Mr Morn," Sorel explained.

"I am Mr Morn's wife," said Leonora, coming up to the door.

"It don't make no difference. You're welcome either way," said the old man kindly.

"I am not quite sure about Laura's room," said Leonora, smiling, "but I think it must have been that side, because one could see from it just the roof of the house with the large barn over there—I have forgotten who lives there."

"The Rogers used to live there," said the woman.

Her father cast another contemptuous look at her, and turning to Sorel with an expression of triumph said, "That's my room. My bed's in there."

He insisted on leading them round to the side of the house, and showed the one small window that must have been Laura's. He and Alexander Sorel looked up at it.

"If you want to see Rogers' roof from up there the woman can get it cleaned up a bit, and I'll take you," said the old man.

"I should like that very much," said Sorel earnestly.

"Hey!" said the man as they went back to the front of the house; "can you get my bit of a room cleaned up by to-morrow for him to see?"

"I can't do it 'fore Friday," said his daughter.

"Will you be coming this way Friday, perhaps?" asked the old man.

"Yes, certainly," said Sorel, taking out a notebook; "and in that case perhaps you would be kind enough to have lunch with me first. Is there an inn near here?"

"Yes," said Leonora, smiling, "the Golden Cock."

"Will you come at one o'clock?" asked Sorel. The old man looked a little puzzled.

"He wants you to have dinner with him in the Cock," said his daughter.

He threw her the accustomed look of scorn, and answered Sorel, weighing his words very carefully, "Yes, I'll come."

Sorel shook his hand excitedly. "Good. Then *le Coq d'Or* at one o'clock."

And they began to walk down the path, Sorel writing in his notebook. At the gate he turned and hurried back to the house.

"Excuse me, I do not know your name," he said, holding his pencil up.

"Tom Burgess," said the man; "that'll find me."

Sorel wrote it down and began to search through all his pockets. At last he handed Tom Burgess his card. "That is my name," he explained.

"Yes, all right," said he; "and if you want to bring the lady along you can. I've nothing much against females' society."

"Yes, thank you," said Sorel.

He and Leonora walked on, past the Rogers' farm where Laura's lover had lived.

"You know, Laura is the only one of his women who was beautiful," said he. "Did he know you when he created her?"

"No," she answered. "I had read the book before I met him."

"She was like you, too," said Sorel, half closing his eyes to imagine Laura with Leonora's face. "She would have been dark and pale, but your forehead is too high—and she was a peasant."

"I have also some peasant blood in me somewhere," said Leonora with a smile.

"Ah, yes," said Sorel, laughing, "but not much."

Tom Burgess's was only the remains of a farm, but the Rogers' farm was large and flourishing. From the road one could see through the trees glimpses of the front of the house, which looked rich and quite imposing. Much farther back there was an enormous barn. Opposite the house, on the other side of the road, were also a few trees, and the road between was white and dusty. Beyond this they went down into a little village and then up the other side. The house where George was born is on the side of a hill.

It is an ugly house built of grey stone, with three windows and a door in the front of it, and a small sloping garden where nothing grows. Leonora did not know who lived there now. The door was closed and they did not see anyone about. They sat down on the short grass at the side of the stony road and looked at the house. They were a little tired. It had become hot, and the road up to the house was steep.

George had lived here with his mother. His father died when he was a child, and she looked after him and all his brothers. Each one of them has been successful, and George is the youngest. His mother was exactly like the women about there, thin, and with a pale, austere face. Leonora saw her only once, when she was dying. She wanted to see the girl George was going to marry. Leonora was playing somewhere not far away, and she came down here to see her. It was in the winter, and it was already dark when she arrived. There was only a lamp in the room. George's mother was lying on the bed perfectly still, her face quite grey. Only her eyes, blue like his, but without any trace of gentleness in them, looked from her son to Leonora and back again. It was impossible to know what she thought; it was only quite easily to be seen that for him she would have let herself be trampled underfoot or torn in pieces. Leonora went back the same evening. It was not until a year after they were married that she came here again and saw the place properly.

She and Alexander Sorel sat for a long time at the side of the road. From here they could see for many miles; but there was nothing but the curves of the roads; the villages were all hidden in the little shallow valleys. The sun was shining, but the sky was a whitish grey. A cart came slowly up the hill, pulled by a white horse walking uncertainly on the loose stones of the road. After this Alexander Sorel and Leonora began to walk down the hill.

On Friday Sorel hurried off to " *le Coq d'Or* " to meet Tom Burgess. Leonora only went to meet them afterwards at the house. When she reached there they had not yet arrived, but in a few minutes they came along the road. Sorel, walking as slowly as he could, listened with absorption to what Tom Burgess was saying. Tom carried a large bunch of roses.

"If you'd been at the dinner you'd have had them sooner," he said, giving them to Leonora with a mixture of severity and magnanimity.

They went upstairs to his bedroom. It was a small room with a small bed, an old rocking-chair, a broken cane chair, and a little window which, though the day was warm, was fast closed. He invited Leonora to sit in the rocking-chair. Sorel seated himself uninvited on the bed.

"I don't often smoke in this room, but you're welcome to to-day if she's got no objection," said Tom Burgess, taking a pipe out of his pocket.

Sorel held his cigarette up in front of him and began to examine the room. He had already told Tom some of the story.

197

"But when Laura slept here the bed must have been over on that side," he said, walking to the back of Leonora's chair, "because she could see the tree from her bed. It must have been that tree. Has any tree been cut down from here, do you think?"

"No," said Tom decidedly.

"Then it must be that one," said Sorel.

"And there's the Rogers' place," said Tom, pointing with one hand and holding his pipe with the other.

"Oh yes," said Sorel, coming to the window. "Can we open it, please?"

They opened it with a little difficulty, and Sorel stood in front of it and looked intently at the roof of the Rogers' farm.

"And you remember," he said, bending down to talk to Tom Burgess, "it was there that Frederick lived and Laura used to stand at the window and look at the roof."

"Aye, poor thing!" said Tom Burgess thoughtfully.

Sorel leaned out of the window as far as he could. "And look," he said, "if she had leaned out like this she could have seen the road along which he must have come here."

Leonora leaned out too, to see, and he held her arm while he turned to look around the room.

"You know," he said, going up to Tom Burgess's chair and looking down at him, "I think you ought to read that book. It's long, but you would like it. I'll send it to you."

"Aye, but I can't read," said Tom, puffing at his pipe.

"Isn't there someone who could read it to you?" asked Leonora. "Your daughter, perhaps?"

"Perhaps she can and perhaps she can't," he said, without enthusiasm, and took another puff at his pipe. Then suddenly leaning out of the window he shouted to someone in the garden. "Hey, Bessie, girl, come up here at once. That's my gran'daughter," he explained. "She can read."

In a few moments a girl of about sixteen came into the room. She wore a print dress with flowers on it and a white pinafore. She was a big girl, rather pretty, but a little stupid-looking, very unlike her mother.

"Can you read?" asked her grandfather abruptly.

She looked from Alexander Sorel to Leonora and back again, and, puzzled and shy, stood silent, with an embarrassed smile on her face.

"Can you read or can't you?" shouted Tom, with the utmost impatience.

"Yes," she said, not taking her eyes off Sorel.

"That is all right then," said Sorel to Tom, and, without looking at her, he took out his little notebook and wrote in it. "I'll send the book down this evening if Mrs Morn will let me send someone, and you can start at once."

"You are going to read a book to me," said Tom impressively to the girl.

She did not answer, but rather stupidly stared at Sorel without moving.

"You're not wanted any more," said Tom. "And tell your mother I'm to have my bed moved against that wall where I can see the tree."

"But, gran'father——" she began.

"Go on," he said; "that's enough."

Sorel turned round to look at her, and with a slight giggle she went out of the room.

Soon afterwards Sorel and Leonora went. As they passed through the kitchen on their way out Tom's daughter asked them to stay to tea. But Tom looked at her with hardly restrained irritation and impatience, and did not seem satisfied until he had shown his guests off the premises without interference of any kind.

"Good-bye, and thank you very much for the roses," said Leonora.

"You're welcome to them," said Tom, and began to walk back to the house.

Bessie, picking gooseberries in the garden,

looked up at them with large eyes as they passed.

Not far from the wall of George Morn's garden there is a wooden bench at the side of the road, and also a few trees, and from this the road curves down through the grass, and a little lower down there is a telegraph-post, its top about on a level with the top of the bench. Morn, Leonora, and Alexander Sorel went towards it one evening after tea. Sorel and Leonora sat on the bench, and Morn stretched himself on the ground opposite them. He was in a very good mood. He put his hat half over his eyes, though there was no sun, and looked lazily down at the road, with a half-smile in his blue eyes. Sorel leaned forward on the bench, and Leonora sat upright but in an attitude of repose, and with a slight smile on her face, one of her hands resting palm upwards on the bench, the other on her lap.

Sorel looked restlessly about him until his attention was caught by the bench itself, on which innumerable names were carved. He studied the names on both sides of him, and afterwards stood up to look at those he had been sitting on.

"I should like to put my name there too," he said, "but I have no knife."

Morn laughed and sat up, with his hat still

half over his eyes, to search his pockets. He handed out a large pocket-knife. "Here," he said, "but don't break the blade; it is a treasured possession."

"Oh, thank you," said Sorel. "Do you mind opening it for me too?"

Morn did so and lay down on his back again. Sorel stooped over the bench and began slowly carving his name. He paused in the middle to say, "I am rather fond of my name, you know."

Leonora bent over to look at it. "He is writing it far bigger than anyone else's," she said, smiling.

"Yes, I am," said Sorel with interest, standing back from the bench to look at his work.

Morn got up from the ground and came over to look. "Yes," he said, smiling down at it. "The truth is, of course, that the names here are usually in pairs and carved at moments when individuality seemed to pale a little before the infinity of love." He looked quickly along the bench. "Why, good Lord, man, this is quite impossible. They are all in pairs but yours. Get up a moment, Leo. Yes, yours is the only single name on the bench. Beware. Venus might take her revenge."

Sorel looked a little distressed.

"Can't you think of a lady to put down too?" said Morn, laughing.

Sorel smiled a little and thought for a moment. His expression became more puzzled.

"I don't know anyone appropriate," he said.

He looked at Leonora for help, but she was laughing. Morn lay down again on the ground.

"I know," said Sorel excitedly. "I can put Laura. You have no objection, have you?"

"My Laura?" said Morn.

"But I had better alter the *o* to *e* in her surname. I can't carve *o*'s," said Sorel. He knelt down before the bench and began to carve.

Morn sat up and looked at his back with an expression of astonishment, but he was also a little amused and pleased.

"I'll have to make her smaller, but I'll put her above me," said Sorel.

They were silent.

At last Sorel got up and carefully brushed his knees.

"Now," he said, sitting on the very edge of the bench by the side of his work, "I have forged an interesting literary document. Your admirers of another generation will come here with notebooks and magnifying-glasses and discover that your Laura was a real person at one time betrothed to one Alexander Sorel."

"It will work more havoc with your biography than with mine," said Morn, laughing.

"I'll put a bracket," said Sorel, and after that he handed the knife back to Morn.

Over on the other side of the house the sun was setting. Already a pale, almost transparent new moon had appeared in the grey sky. As the twilight came the road looked whiter in the middle of the dark ground, and the telegraph-post like a black line.

Morn lay without moving. Sorel, his light mood suddenly vanished, with his arms tightly folded, gazed intently at the ground in front of him. Leonora sat quite still on the bench and looked down half smiling at her hands.

Beyond the telegraph-post the road was hidden for a few hundred yards, and then it curved again into sight. Now the sun had quite set and it grew darker. Sorel, looking up from the ground, saw someone walking along the road in the distance—a man with a hat and a thick stick. From there he looked quite black, almost a silhouette.

Sorel, with his head bent forward, wrinkled his forehead to look upwards at him, and he watched him intently until he disappeared in the hollow of the road. Then he bent down and felt the ground with his fingers. He turned to Leonora.

"The grass is damp," he said anxiously in a whisper. "You ought not to let him lie on it."

Leonora looked at him for a moment without answering. "He is very strong, you know," she said, "and quite used to it." She put her other hand down on the bench and looked across at the road.

"He'll catch cold," said Sorel, and, getting up, bent over Morn and touched his shoulder. "The grass is wet," he said.

There was no answer.

"Why, would you believe it," said Sorel in surprise, "he is fast asleep, and it is the sleep of a good conscience."

Morn opened his eyes and pushed his hat off.

"The grass is wet," said Sorel, still with his hand on Morn's shoulder.

Morn laughed.

Sorel looked at him without smiling, but as he did so he caught sight of the same man climbing the road towards them. "It is Mr Burgess," he said, and, leaving Morn, hurried down the road to meet him. They came up together, Tom Burgess talking and Sorel listening, walking slowly with his head bent.

"Evening," said Tom.

"Hullo!" said Morn. "How d'ye do?"

"*I'm* all right," said Tom.

"Won't you sit down, Mr Burgess?" said Leonora.

"Thank you, I will," he said. "I've been

visiting an old chap I used to know. *He* won't last long."

He sat down on the bench and Sorel on the other side of him.

"Who is that?" asked Morn, turning over on his side.

"Old Harris," said Tom. "Used to work for Rogers."

"Yes, I knew him very well," said Morn. "Dying, is he?"

"Aye, dying, if anyone was," said Tom in a depressed voice.

"I'd better call in and see him," said Morn. "Poor old chap!" He looked down at the grass.

"Are you reading the book?" asked Sorel, breaking in.

"Yes," said Tom, pulling out his pipe. "But my gran'daughter Bessie's a fool of a girl."

"Why, can't she read after all?" asked Sorel anxiously.

Tom's expression changed to one of the deepest scorn. "Oh aye, she can *read*," he said at last. And then turning to Sorel he said, "The girl's taken a fancy to you now. Wants to know what your work is. She thinks you must be a lawyer," and he puffed disgustedly at his pipe.

Sorel was immensely amused. He laughed. "And do you know what I really do?" he said to Tom delightedly.

"No," said Tom.

"Well, when I am in a good temper I compose music, and when I am not I don't."

"Yes, I'll tell her that then," said Tom, looking a trifle bored. He turned to Leonora and said, "And how are you getting along now?"

"Very well, Mr Burgess," she said; "the place suits me, I think."

"Perhaps it's the first time you've been here," said Tom, putting his head slightly on one side and covering his curiosity with a casual air.

"Why, good Lord, no," said Morn. "We came down here about a year after we were married, and stayed three or four months with Mrs Semley up at the farm. Surely you met her then? I came to see you."

"Aye, aye, I remember *you*," said Tom, "but I don't remember seeing her. And she's the same one, is she?"

"Yes, the same one," said Morn, laughing.

"And I suppose you didn't find her round about here?" said Tom.

"No," said Morn; "I found her in London."

"Aye, the women about here aren't up to much. When I married my missus it wasn't for her looks."

"My mother was a wonderful woman," said Morn. "But perhaps you're right. She wasn't really beautiful."

"But she's a beauty," said Tom, indicating Leonora with his finger.

She smiled. "You are very kind," she said ; "but I am getting older, you know."

Sorel laughed.

"But your granddaughter is rather a pretty girl, Mr Burgess; don't you think so?" said Leonora, smiling again.

"Oh, her!" said Tom, and became silent. "Her father wasn't from round here," he added.

It had become much darker. The moon shed a little light, but the road and the telegraph-post were scarcely distinguishable any longer. Tom Burgess took his pipe out of his mouth and knocked the ashes out of it against the bench.

"Well, I must be going," he said, getting up.

"It has got so cold," said Leonora, pulling a thin scarf around her shoulders and shivering a little. They walked up the road past the wall of the garden.

"I'll be getting on now," said Tom at the gate.

"I'll come part of the way with you," said Sorel. And they walked together along the road.

At the side of the road some water trickled over the stones. The light, suddenly turned on in Morn's room, sent one long ray after them. Before they turned down the path into the valley someone came along the road towards them.

"Is that you, gran'father?" said Bessie's voice out of the darkness.

"Aye," he said sulkily.

"We thought you was lost, and I had to come after you," she said, coming to a standstill in front of him.

"H'm," he said, walking to the side past her. And they walked on again, Bessie following quietly behind them, her eyes fixed on Sorel's back. Sorel went with him right as far as the house, but he stopped at the gate.

"You can have a bit of supper if you come in," said Tom.

"No, thank you very much," said Sorel, and shaking hands with him he turned to go. It was only then he remembered that Bessie was the girl who had taken a fancy to him. He turned round again, but only in time to see her following the old man up the path. But when they got to the door the light from the kitchen showed her turning round to look at him. And after that he walked home.

The river is not very far away from here. There is a very gradual slope for about a mile from the house, then there are a few ferns here and there and numbers of big stones, and then the river, with at that point three small, bare islands in it. It is fairly wide but not at all deep, except in one or two places. But these

are holes in the river-bed. Everywhere else
one can see the stones quite distinctly, and in
some places the water breaking over a larger
stone. There are probably no fish in it now,
though Morn says he used to catch trout there
when he was a boy. There are no trees anywhere, only far away on the other side of the
river there are about six trees growing all
crowded together. And in one of Morn's novels
two lovers used to meet here on this bank and
walk up and down by the river. So Leonora
brought Sorel here also.

That day it was not hot; Leonora wore a coat,
and Sorel, because his own coat was too thick,
wore a thin green raincoat of Morn's which
reached almost to his boots. They walked the
short distance slowly, and at last sat down
on a large grey stone, like a low oval table,
a few yards from the river's edge. Leonora
sat in silence, and Sorel looked straight in
front of him across the river. His coat was
buttoned up at the neck, and his cap rather
hid the upper part of his face. In fact, the
coat made him look a little ridiculous. It
was particularly cold. There was no wind,
but it seemed colder down there than up by
the house. Leonora looked for a moment at
Sorel's feet and at the bottom of her husband's
coat.

"George wore that coat when I came down here first," she said. "It rained nearly the whole time we were here. We came to see all these places in the rain."

"How much had he written by then?" asked Sorel.

"Only three," said Leonora, "besides the early stories, which are really bad. He was already over forty."

"If he had written only the first stories would you have married him?"

"I do not know," she said. "There was no promise of any kind in them."

She looked up and smiled, but Sorel was still gazing intently across the river. She looked beyond him up the slope and smiled again.

"Do look at that sheep meditating on human nature," she said.

Sorel turned round to see. A sheep was standing near looking at them with absorbed interest. Sorel looked at its thin, white, mild, intellectual face.

"Ah, this is positively sublime!" he said, laughing excitedly, and, getting up from the stone, he walked in his long coat towards the sheep, holding out his hand enticingly.

The sheep, still looking at him, turned to retreat, and then ran up the slope and, stopping higher up near a flat stone, resumed its contemplation. Sorel came back laughing to the stone and sat down again.

"There. That is how I see life," he said— "two people sitting on a stone by a river with stones in it, and a sheep looking at them. Ah, in that, you know, there is something ineffably tragic and also very agreeable."

Leonora smiled, but looked into the distance up the river. Sorel, instead of speaking, looked at her. The scarf of her coat was wound tightly round her neck, and sitting there on the stone she looked thin and tall, and also perhaps a little old. Sorel looked at her. Then he leaned forward on the stone and covered his face with his hands. For some reason he began to feel extraordinarily depressed. Nothing moved around, the sheep had gone, there were no birds. Perhaps right beneath the stone on which they sat there were ants. The sky was grey, and soon a soft drizzling rain began to fall.

"It has begun to rain," said Leonora gently. Sorel took his hands from his eyes and looked up. "Yes," he said, and stood up.

"No, don't go unless you want to," she said. "The rain suits this place."

He looked down at her. "But your hair," he said; "you have no hat."

"It will not hurt it. Rain is very good for hair."

"Is it?" he said with interest, and put his cap

in his pocket. "Now there is also equality," he added.

She smiled. "No, you will catch cold."

He sat and watched the fine rain fall on the water of the river.

"It rained the day Annie sat here for hours waiting," said Leonora. "Do you remember? Those women were always waiting for somebody. Now in these days there is nothing to wait for."

"Yes, one almost feels that she is still sitting upon that rock in the rain," he said. "What would she have been dressed in?"

"She was in service," said Leonora. "I suppose a black dress and an old coat over it. I am afraid it is the kind of rain that makes one very wet," she added after a pause.

Sorel stood up and took her hand to help her up from her seat. They walked away through the grey drizzling rain, leaving two dry places where they had sat on the stone.

One day Mr James Carmen, who had been a friend of Morn's since they were boys, called on him.

"I knew you were in residence from the papers," he said, sitting down and passing his white handkerchief over his forehead. "Is the missus here too?"

"Yes," said Morn. "This is excellent, you

know. How long can you stay? Whisky and
soda?"

"Yes, better make it weak though," he said.
"Only to-night. Did you ever meet the man
my sister Annie married?"

"No, I don't think so. How is she?"

"He has just died suddenly. The world is
better off in consequence; but, of course, the
poor girl is upset. I have been up to see her,
and I am on my way back. There are a number
of business matters to attend to. That is why
I mustn't get drunk."

"At any rate it is good to see you to-night,"
said Morn, putting his papers one by one into
the drawer of the table. "Couldn't you come
back some time this summer?"

"Perhaps I could," said James Carmen.
"Anyone here besides you and Leo?"

"Yes," said Morn, "Alexander Sorel."

"Oh!" said Carmen, taking two cigars very
carefully out of his pocket and handing one
to Morn. "Here, this is a very valuable cigar;
smoke it thoughtfully. And who is Alexander
Sorel? He wasn't mentioned in the paper?"

"No, we don't use the same papers," said
Morn, laughing. "Alexander Sorel the com-
poser."

"Never heard of him," said James Carmen.
"What's he like? Daft?"

Morn paused in lighting his cigar, opened his eyes very wide in pretended surprise, and slowly winked.

"Oh!" said Carmen, laughing, and showing his very white teeth.

Sorel and Leonora were out and did not return until after tea. Sorel sat on the edge of a chair and looked at James Carmen attentively. But Carmen talked to Leonora.

"I'm said to be drinking myself to death," he said, looking at her with solemnity.

She smiled.

"George will leave a lot of books behind him," he continued, "I a lot of bills for whisky. There's no difference."

Morn looked at him with a smile in his blue eyes.

"Go on," said Sorel, leaning forward earnestly.

Carmen turned to look at him. "Go on with what?" he asked abruptly.

"With what you were saying," said Sorel.

Carmen began to shake with invisible laughter and held his white handkerchief up to his mouth. Sorel smiled in perplexity and looked inquiringly at Leonora.

"Will you let me play the Greek dance to Mr Carmen after dinner?" she said. "I should like him to hear it. It is something of Mr Sorel's," she said to Carmen.

"But it is not yet finished," said Sorel, turning to Carmen anxiously and apologetically.

"The first part is finished," said Leonora.

"All right; let's have it," said Carmen, putting his white handkerchief in his pocket.

After dinner they went into the drawing-room. Morn, talking to Carmen over his shoulder, fetched Leonora's 'cello out of its case in the corner and she sat down and took it. Sorel sat at the piano and looked round at her. The 'cello rested against her white dress. Her head was bent in an attitude of strength and the position of her arms gave her shoulders breadth. There is something strange about a woman playing the 'cello. Women like sibyls, with strength like iron, do not exist any more. Goddesses now are whisps of things. But there are still women who play the 'cello. She began to play the Greek dance.

All the time while Sorel played, while the melody fell wailing away from his fingers, and then at the end when only the dark rhythm of the dance was left, he could see Leonora quite clearly in the air in front of him. And when it was over he looked round in time to see her with her head still bent carrying the bow slowly away. He stood up.

"I think I will go on with the second part," he said. "Please excuse me." He shook hands with Carmen, and then said to Leonora on the way out, "There isn't any ink in my room."

She went into Morn's room and came back bringing a little square green inkwell. Sorel took it and went away carrying it very carefully, so that it should not spill.

"I hope *you* are not going to retire to worship art in secret?" said Carmen.

"No," she said; "I am going to walk round the garden first."

"I'll come with you," said he, moving his empty glass to the middle of the table.

"What did you think of the music?" she asked.

"Oh, the Lord knows!" said Carmen. "Are you fed up with this place yet?"

"It is not so very desolate," she said.

"I don't think much of your garden," he said.

"No; that is rather desolate by moonlight, I admit."

The moon was not full, but its light fell on the garden and on the house, and the garden wall cast a black shadow. Leonora walked first along the path, stopping sometimes to speak of something. He stood beside her, and pressed his white handkerchief over his forehead, though it was certainly no longer hot. He looked around him uneasily.

"Here am I in the moonlight with a pretty

217

woman, and the wife of my best friend into the bargain," he thought, "and I don't feel like making love to her. There is something wrong with me, or that little fool of a man has spoiled my digestion."

"It is a pity the garden is so ugly," said Leonora.

"I am not surprised," he said. "The place must have been full of stones. I threw about a hundredweight in here when I was a boy."

"Yes, I believe it was full of stones," said Leonora; "George carried them all out. Why did you do that?"

"I don't know. George threw a lot of them in himself," said Carmen in a depressed voice. "I suppose it was to annoy somebody. There doesn't seem much sense in it now. It seemed a sensible thing to do then. I suppose there is no sense in anything I do now either."

"One cannot know that," said Leonora. She stooped down to a straggling rose tree whose roses, with the moon shining on them, looked almost blue. "Would you like a blue rose?" she said. "Put it under your pillow and in the morning it will be pink."

"Like litmus paper," said Carmen. "See if there is any acid in me. Is alcohol an acid?"

"I don't know," she said, smiling. "Must you really go to-morrow?"

"Yes," he said.

"George likes having you here very much. Won't you come again this summer? He won't go on working at the present rate indefinitely. Then you could have a good holiday here together. Only don't throw stones into the garden."

"How long are you staying?" he asked doubtfully.

"Until October," she answered.

"And what about your little friend?"

"He," said Leonora, looking up at the sky, "he stays only a few weeks longer."

"She's a darned beautiful woman," thought Carmen, looking at her. She was in white, and her face was white too, except for her dark eyes.

"There is nothing so entirely without form as the moon at this stage," she said. "Nothing on earth. Have you noticed?"

"I'll try to come some time in September," he said, as they walked back to the house.

"Yes, do come," she said. "We shall both be delighted."

Alexander Sorel did not go to bed until it was beginning to get light, and he did not come down in time for breakfast. But he came down immediately afterwards. James Carmen had already gone. Sorel went for a walk by himself. It was a fine day, and he wore a light suit and no hat, and went jauntily along the road. By the time he had reached a wooden seat at the side of the road upon the grass his state of mind had reached such a degree of idyllic happiness that he did not exhaust himself in any further effort, but sat down on the seat. He put one hand on his knee, crossed his legs, and swung one of them back and fore a little. It was a very fine day. The sky was blue, with round white clouds in it very high up. A few harebells, the exact blue of the sky, grew on their threadlike green stems near one of the legs of the bench. The sun shone on his head.

A girl in a pink dress was coming along the road in the distance, but she turned off on to the grass and walked there from one place to another, apparently without aim, and stooped down to the grass. Sorel looked at her. He felt exceedingly light-hearted, and thought over a few bars of *L'Après-Midi d'un Faune* to himself. The girl, describing like a bird illogical circles on the grass, came gradually nearer to him, and at last stood facing him on the opposite side of the road, with her mouth slightly open and the under-lip drooping. He saw that it was Bessie, and that she had been picking harebells. He smiled across at her. She gave a shy laugh and put her head down, raising one shoulder as she did so and keeping her eyes on him.

"Come over here," he called, smiling.

She laughed again, but came slowly across the road and sat down on the bench at the other end.

"And you have been picking flowers?" he said.

"Yes. But these here die as soon as they're picked. It's because they've got thin stalks."

"Yes, extraordinarily thin stalks," agreed Sorel.

Bessie bent down to put the harebells under the bench in the shadow of her legs. "It's not so hot there," she explained.

"No," he said. "How is your grandfather to-day?"

"All right."

"And what do you do all day?" he asked.

"I look after the chickens and do the house, but my mother sells the eggs. To-day she's gone to market, so there isn't much to do."

"And do you like it?"

"Like what, do you mean?" she asked.

"Do you like your life here?"

"But I live here," she said. "Only I'd like to travel."

"To travel!" said Sorel, laughing. "But where?"

"I'd like to go to France," she said.

"What would you do there?"

"Go into service."

"Oh," he said thoughtfully.

"Have you travelled, please?" she asked.

"Travelled?" he said. "Well, yes, I've been to a lot of places. Last year I went to Greece."

"Have you been to France?" she asked.

"Yes," he said.

She looked longingly at the ground.

"I don't think it is a very good idea of yours," he said. "I think this place is quite as nice." He smiled down at her.

She giggled again shyly and began to scrape her boot on the ground.

"I must go," she said reluctantly. "Gran'-father'll want his dinner."

She picked up the harebells and walked past Sorel, then she turned back and put the flowers on top of his hand.

"You can have them if you like," she said.

"Oh, thank you very much," said Sorel, and turned his attention to gathering them into a bunch again. But he did so in time to shake hands with her, and then he carried them very carefully home, bending now and then to pick up one that unfastened itself from his hand. And he had them put in a vase in his room.

That evening he sat up there at the table before the window and began to play with his pen. The harebells were on the table, but he moved them to another part of the room. Outside the twilight was beginning almost imperceptibly to creep like a grey transparent cloud over the grass. He could see a very long way from his window. And with the twilight great grey shadows seemed to come from each curve and valley and walk about over the earth. He looked at them, and began to turn the lines of the manuscript sheet in front of him into little squares. When he looked up again it was much darker outside; there were lights in houses here and there. He turned on the light at his table.

There was a knock at the door and Leonora came in.

"Forgive me for disturbing you," she said. "I could copy the second part to-night if you have it. Is it quite finished?"

"Yes; you can have it now. I am doing the third part," he said, indicating the manuscript paper.

She looked down at the three bands of little squares without smiling. He did not notice it.

"You shall play it in October," he said.

"I like it very much," said Leonora.

He wrinkled his forehead and looked down at the manuscript sheets doubtfully, but he put his hand on hers, which rested on the table, and ran his fingers across the stone of her ring before he took his hand away.

"And the second part?" she asked.

He walked over to the table on which the harebells were and opened a drawer. He took some collars out and laid them on the table, and then carefully brought the manuscript from the bottom of the drawer. It came out with a tie hanging to it. He gave her the music and began to tidy the drawer.

"I'll copy the piano part too, and then my copy can go to the publisher instead of this," she said, looking over it.

"You can keep the original if you would like to," he said, pushing the drawer closed.

"I should like it very much," she said, and walked to the door holding the music sheets up against her as she examined the last of them. "I like so much to have to copy it before I play it."

"Leonora!" he said suddenly.

"Yes," she said, turning.

He drew his hand across his forehead and looked at her with his head bent forward.

"I was going to ask you to stay here and talk to me," he said, "but I had better get on with this."

"Would you like some coffee?" she asked.

"Ah, please," he said, and sat down at the table.

He wrote a few bars and looked at the darkness outside.

George knocked at the door and came in. "I met your coffee coming upstairs," he said, putting it on the table. He looked out through the window. "It's going to rain to-morrow."

"Can you tell the weather?" asked Sorel.

"I know more or less how it behaves in this part of the country," said Morn. "I liked that Greek dance of yours last night."

"Did you really?" said Sorel. "That pleases me very much."

"Enough sugar?" said Morn.

Sorel hurriedly sipped the coffee. "Yes, quite, thank you."

Morn took the sugar-basin and went out of the room and down the stairs. He put some of the lumps of sugar into his pocket and put the basin on the bottom pillar of the balusters. He put his hand on the door-handle of the drawing-room where Leonora had begun the copying. He listened for a moment. She was whistling softly, almost under her breath. But he did not go in. He walked into his study, moved one or two papers on the table, and went and stood by the window and looked out into the darkness. The dead rose tree was just distinguishable on the lawn. He began to eat a lump of sugar. He stayed there a few minutes,

and afterwards he went into the dining-room.
But there was nothing there. He went out and
stood at the bottom of the stairs, half meaning
to go up again, but instead he took up the
sugar-basin, which was still there, and carried it
into the kitchen. There was no one there. The
fire was still in, but it needed stirring. He sat
down in the basket chair and took up the poker.
At the side of the fireplace was a calendar with
a photograph of a beauty spot in Great Britain
over each month. After he had poked the fire
he took the calendar down and ate his sugar,
and looked at the photographs with interest.

And a few days afterwards he heard Leonora
going out by herself and ran out to the door to
stop her.

"I want to read to you what I have done this
week," he said. "When can you come?"

"Now," she said, beginning to unbutton her
coat.

"No. I tell you what," he said. "I will
bring it out and come with you."

He went into his room to fetch it, and came
back with the papers sticking out of his coat
pocket.

They walked along the road and up to the
seat where Sorel had carved his name. They
sat down there and Morn began to read, and
as he finished each page he pushed it into his

coat pocket again, but some of them he put
on the bench with a large stone on them. The
wind rustled them a bit but they did not
blow away.

She looked at the grass all around with the
shadows of the grey clouds upon it, and bent
her head and listened to his voice. The monotonous hard simplicity of the words and of his
reading deepened and darkened into tragedy.
Through the brightness of the sun shining on
the grass, and through the shadows of the clouds
which implied the sun's presence, the dark, hard
austerity of the earth seemed to penetrate as a
bright sun through a curtain of black gauze.
The woman of the novel, in her black dress with
her pale, hard face, seemed to walk over the land,
her feet below the sunlight, resting on this under-
surface.

For Leonora the scene and the book and her
husband's voice blended into this one impression.
It was not a tragedy that sweeps to its climax
with hysterical and ironic laughter. She sat
quite still upon the bench looking down. She
was very conscious of her own stillness. She felt
that her soul was being touched by the emotions
of a woman infinitely far away, in another time
and in another world. There was nothing
equally in them both but that they were both
women.

As the story fell slowly down from its climax Morn suddenly stopped reading and said, "Damnation!"

She looked up. Alexander Sorel was coming along the road towards them.

"It doesn't matter," she said. "You can go on from where you are."

"No. Look here," he said, "I can't read it to him. Wait until it is out."

"But why?" she asked. "It would please him very much."

"No, I'd rather not," he said. "You shall see the rest to-night." He looked at her questioningly.

"Yes, it has moved me very deeply," she said, and looked down at the ground.

He pushed the remaining sheets and those under the stone into his pocket as Sorel came up.

Sorel walked quickly, his hands in his pockets, his head bent forward. He wore no hat, and his hair was blown about and his forehead quite damp. He looked very hot. He came and sat down on the bench between Leonora and Morn without speaking.

Morn had forgiven him the interruption. "You look warm," he said.

"Yes," said Sorel. "I have been walking quickly. I like the sensation of moving very quickly. There is something even sublime about trees and houses streaming past me."

"Do you walk as quickly as that?" asked Leonora, smiling.

He looked sideways up at her with a look of tired perplexity. "Oh yes, I think so," he said. "Quite quickly enough to get the sensation."

They were silent. The sun, half hidden by a cloud, shone a little on the trunk of the tree just above Sorel's shoulder. He rested his head on his hands and suddenly began to weep. He hastily reached for his handkerchief with one hand. Morn looked at him and then at Leonora with an embarrassed grimace. She was looking calmly at Sorel. But afterwards she touched his shoulder with her hand and said, "What is the matter?"

"Oh, my God, I don't know," said Sorel, looking up and suddenly beginning to laugh. He put his hands back in his pockets.

After that they became silent again. Morn, smiling a little to himself, contemplated with an inward eye the sheets of manuscript in his coat pocket. Leonora sat upright on the bench looking down at her hands, turned palm upwards on her lap. She was thinking of the woman in George's novel again. And Sorel, with his head stretched back, looked up at the sky, his forehead wrinkled and the same look of tired perplexity on his face. They stayed there a long time.

In the evening Leonora went on reading the novel. When she had finished all that was yet written she put the papers in the drawer of the table, and putting over her shoulder a coat of George's that lay on the chair she stepped over the low sill of the window and walked across the grass past the dead rose tree to the gate. As she opened it she saw that there was someone standing at the side against the wall.

"Who is there?" she asked.

A girl slipped out into the light from the window. It was Bessie, and she carried half behind her back a large bunch of sweet-peas.

"Do you want anyone?" asked Leonora.

"No, miss," said Bessie.

"Are you just going for a walk?" said Leonora, beginning to walk on.

The girl did not answer.

"Good-night," said Leonora.

"Here, miss," said Bessie, and held out the bunch of flowers.

Leonora took them. "Are they for Mr Sorel?" she asked.

Bessie reddened. "No, miss; for you."

"For me?" said Leonora. "That is very kind of you. Are they from your grandfather?"

"Yes—no—from me," said Bessie.

"Thank you very much," said Leonora.

Bessie hesitated a moment and then ran down the road.

Leonora opened the gate again and went in. She carried the sweet-peas up to Sorel's room and put them in the vases, but afterwards she took off George's coat and carried it back to his room.

After that there was only one day that is worth remembering before Sorel went away. It was a very warm day, the best in the whole summer. He and Leonora went early after breakfast for a walk. The long, straight road shone quite white in the sun. It led right away from the house and sloped gradually, not over a hill but over a little mound. Here grew very many harebells, and Leonora and Sorel sat down on the light dry grass. That day there was not a cloud. The sun shone silently.

"Will you let me take off my shoes?" asked Sorel.

She nodded.

He leaned forward and took them off, and moved his toes about in his green socks. Then he measured their length flat on the ground. A harebell was growing up just by the side, and it bent like a Lilliputian princess over the foot

of this Gulliver. He looked down at it. Sorel's
eyes were not blue but a kind of pale greyish
green.

"Those sweet-peas in my room are very nice,
but I like harebells better," he said.

"Mr Burgess's granddaughter brought them,"
said Leonora. "She gave them to me, but I
think they were intended for you."

"Oh, did she really?" said Sorel, looking up,
but afterwards he turned his attention to the
little harebell again.

Leonora sat without a movement and looked
down along the road. The houses here and
there seemed from up here very small. In one
of them George was writing. Sorel's empty
shoes stood on the grass beside him. He
arranged them very carefully toe to toe.

"My shoes look extraordinarily large when I
am not in them," he observed.

"Yes," she said, looking at them and at his
feet. "Do you get them a size too large for
you?"

"I don't think so," he said.

They were silent again. Sorel leaned back on
his elbows on the grass and looked up at the pale
blue sky. There was not the slightest breath of
wind, and not a sound even of a grasshopper.

"All the time I have been here I have not
seen a butterfly," he said suddenly.

"Nor have I," said Leonora.

He moved his shoulders sideways along the grass until his head nearly touched her. He looked up at her backwards.

"Leonora," he said, "do you know I am always alone?"

She looked down at him and did not smile. "So am I," she said.

He looked again up at the sky, but without knowing it he had grasped a fold of her white dress in his hand.

"I thought a lot about you when I wrote the second part of the dance," he said.

"And do I mean for you strength and the spirit that reflects?" she said.

He sat up and looked at her. She still looked down along the road towards the house, her dress, pulled tightly by his hand, stretched out in front of her, not like a dress, but like stone.

"No," he said, "no."

He lay down again on the grass and let her dress go.

"I can't get on with the third part," he said.

"Perhaps when you leave here you will," she said.

"Yes, I suppose so."

They stayed there a long time, he with his eyes wide open looking up at the sky. Afterwards he put on his shoes and they went, and one could see for a long time where they had rested by the pressed-down grass.

A few days afterwards he went away. Morn carried his bag downstairs and out to the gate. He came hurrying along the path looking worried, carrying his grey gloves in his hand.

"Leonora," he said, "I have forgotten to say good-bye to Mr Burgess. Please go there this afternoon for me, and tell him he can keep the book as a present. It is the first edition, and my name is written in it," he added. "His great-grandchildren will be able to sell it."

He turned to Morn and shook hands with him and thanked him, but all the time he looked anxiously about him, as he did before when he came there first. Morn remained standing by the dead rose tree.

Sorel got into the car. "Don't forget Mr Burgess," he said. "And if I have forgotten anything, please be so kind as to send it after me."

He pressed Leonora's hands. Then the car drove away and Leonora turned and walked back along the path.